CHAINSAW HONEYMOON

PRAISE FOR CHAINSAW HONEYMOON

"In this tale of a daughter literally trying to scare her estranged parents back together, Steven Ramirez combines the horror/slasher film and literature genres with the light comedy/romance of a Cary Grant film. Both genres present challenges on their own. What is amazing about Chainsaw Honeymoon is how Ramirez surmounts both of these demands. Added to these accomplishments is his ability to present the viewpoint of a fourteen-year-old girl. In the form of Ruby, Ramirez imparts to readers all the confusion brought about by puberty; the emotional neediness camouflaged by sarcasm; the obsession and continuing frustration with boys; and the bonds female teenagers forge with one another."

— INDIEREADER

"Whether your favorite form is surreal, tongue-in-cheek, word play or hysterical, you'll find ample portions of each to keep you laughing. The pace is fast, told from several points of view, and full of surprises that make for an unforgettable read."

— READERS' FAVORITE

"The writing throughout the novel is sharp and smart, depicting the City of Angels like a key character, setting the stage for the plot to unravel, while also capturing some of the strangest sides of the film industry. Ruby is a precocious and fascinating narrator, and the supporting cast of friends, actors, and unexpected allies drive this novel forward."

— Self-Publishing Review

BOOKS BY STEVEN RAMIREZ

Jane Doe Cycle

Brandon's Last Words

Faithless

Sarah Greene Mysteries

The Girl in the Mirror

House of the Shrieking Woman

The Blood She Wore

Tell Me When I'm Dead

Tell Me When I'm Dead

Dead Is All You Get

Even The Dead Will Bleed

Other Books

Chainsaw Honeymoon

Come As You Are: A Short Novel and Nine Stories

Come As You Are: A Novella

Glass Highway
Los Angeles, CA
stevenramirez.com

Publisher's Note: This is a work of fiction. Names, characters, places, and incidents are a product of the author's imagination. Locales and public names are sometimes used for atmospheric purposes. Any resemblance to actual people, living or dead, or to businesses, companies, events, institutions, or locales is completely coincidental.

Chainsaw Honeymoon / Steven Ramirez.—1st ed.
ISBN-13: 978-0-9990791-4-0
Library of Congress Control Number: 2018900313

Edited by Shannon A. Thompson
Cover design by Deborah Bradseth
Special thanks to Sheila Cicchi for the Minnesota slang

CHAINSAW HONEYMOON

STEVEN RAMIREZ

Glass Highway
LOS ANGELES, CALIFORNIA

For Corinne. It had to be you.

"This is the most fantastic story I've ever heard. And every word of it's true, too. That's the fantastic part of it."

— *Plan 9 from Outer Space*

CHAINSAW HONEYMOON

1

"I just can't take no pleasure in killing."

— THE TEXAS CHAIN SAW MASSACRE (1974)

They never get it right in the movies, the things going through your head at the very moment your killer bursts into the room, ready to chop up the party guests—including you and your family—into kibble. It isn't your life flashing before your eyes like a silent movie or your favorite stuffed animal or the car you thought you'd own when you turned eighteen. And it isn't the realization that you'll never marry and have kids or visit Europe.

Nope. It's something random. Like socks. In my case, it was a nonspecific cheeseburger—juicy and rare—with crispy fries in a cute, little, shiny metal cup. Oh, and a tall vanilla shake with twin barber pole straws. The thought of never experiencing that meal again brought down on me a deep sorrow difficult to describe in words. All I can say is, it felt like getting clobbered with Thor's hammer.

I can tell you what the movies *do* get right, though.

Everything. Slows. Down. And the air gets thicker than fire-weed honey. You can't move because your fear has you trapped like a mosquito in amber. So, you might as well relax, *jefe*. The entire experience is like a dream really, only you know in your soul it's not a dream—but you wish it was, because the reality that's about to turn you into fish food is too horrible to imagine. And I'm all about horrible, so.

They say in dream time you can live an entire life in only a few minutes. If this was a dream, I wished I could wake up, hug my dog, and pound down a whole package of Pecan Sandies. But as I cowered against the wall, half-broken from being flung back like a shaving cream pie in a silent comedy, I wondered why I thought I could take on my nightmare of an enemy. It's preposterous. I mean, I can't even do ten push-ups! But there I was. And there *he* was.

Chainsaw Chuck.

Okay, so Chainsaw Chuck was the crazed killer I invented, only he was no longer a character in my machinima project, and he only recently had acquired that name, courtesy of a movie I was involved with. So much to explain, so little time. Anyways, this creature was flesh and blood, and he had come to kill his creator. Standing in front of me, big and scary, he wore his signature black high-crown, wide-brim hat—designed by me—and his weapon of choice dangled darkly from his left hand. An impressive monster, if I do say so myself.

Staring at me in surly silence, he gathered himself up and revved the deadly chainsaw, which echoed up and down the shadowy corridor. Sort of like what old dudes on Harleys do when a pretty girl walks by. I could see his teeth, which were gray and pointy, and I could feel his hot, deadly breath. Yep, I was going to die for sure. *It wasn't fair!* Ed Wood, our over-caffeinated Shih Tzu, had followed me from the party and stood between the killer and me, barking like a maniac and tearing at his long black duster. I guessed my dog's fate was pretty much sealed, too. At least, I wouldn't die alone.

Why? That is the question. No normal person would have chased this demon, let alone tried to take him down. That only ever happens in the movies—bad movies. No, in real life they would have gathered up their family and their two best friends and would've run like hell out of the stinking building while dialing 911 on their phone. Common sense, people!

Not me. I had to be the hero.

Where was I? Oh, yeah. I sat on the floor, frozen, my knees tucked up under my chin. It was like I weighed a million pounds. Maybe if I made myself really, really small —like Ant-Man—he wouldn't see me. Everything was slow and dreamy now, like "Last Kiss" by Pearl Jam. I love that song.

I noticed the gleam in Chainsaw Chuck's tiny, savage eyes, and I knew this was it. The End. *Fin. Fine.* But I couldn't help but feel this *was* a dream after all. A pernicious nightmare I was incapable of awakening from. Talk about your random thoughts. For some reason, I was picturing that poor idiot replicant Leon from *Blade Runner*. I could hear him in my head now, his eyes intense, his voice close and menacing as he was about to shove his fingers through Deckard's eye holes.

"Wake up! Time to die."

"Wakey, wakey, eggs and bakey."

— HOUSE OF 1000 CORPSES

Horror is my life. Seriously. My idea of a Best Birthday Ever is to be at the Nuart when they screen the original 1977 version of *Suspiria* (we don't show movies in LA—we "screen" them), munching on a large popcorn—thank you very much—drenched in Log Cabin syrup (I have to smuggle that in), and guzzling a Jarritos Tamarind soda (also smuggled in). Next stop, The Apple Pan for a steakburger—rare with extra onions, please —and a single cup of black coffee, accompanied by a slice of warm apple pie topped with a humungous scoop of Danish vanilla ice cream.

What, too hipster, you say? Hey, I'm talking *burgers* here, people, not artisanal lawn furniture. Hipster, puh-leeze... Well, maybe a little.

Here are some things you should know about me. So, my name. Ruby Navarro. I turned fourteen this past March and somehow made it through ninth grade with a 3.85 GPA. I'm an Aries, which means I am eager, dynamic, quick, and competitive. At least, according to those astrology websites, which I never visit. Mostly. I am also precocious and well read, which explains why I skipped a grade. My two best friends in the whole world—and the ones I would totally take a bullet for—are Claire Tran and Diego Rivera.

Claire is like my sister. Her Vietnamese name is Hang, which means "moon." She'll be fifteen at the end of November, which makes her a Sagittarius. She is inquisitive and energetic, and a traveler of the Zodiac. Diego, a Leo, will be fifteen in August, which makes him almost "driverable." He is dramatic, creative, and outgoing. Not that I believe in any of that astrology jazz. But I will say the three of us make an awesome team. Claire and Diego are the only people in the universe who get me.

Back to me. I sleep like the dead, truly. It's a medical fact. When I was a baby, doctors at Elm Street Pediatric Research for Effective Sleep Outcomes—or ESPRESO—which is a tad ironic, if you stop to think about it—had marveled at how vampire-like my "mimis" was. I mean, I hardly breathed. And when I did, it was in these huge, irregular, gulping gasps that scared my parents half to death.

According to my mother, the pediatrician had recommended everything: swaddling, SIDS pillows, behavior modification. Even a slowly spinning mobile hung over my crib, which, instead of rainbows and unicorns, featured tiny, gleaming silver daggers and gently tinkled the theme to *The Addams Family* television show. Yeah, Mom's a "horrorista," too, which is probably where I get it. Anyways, none of it worked. So my parents, the long-suffering Alan and Stacey Navarro, eventually gave up, and...surprise! I'm still here. Moving on.

SCHOOL HAD ALREADY LET OUT—WHOO-HOO!—AND summer was upon us. It was Tuesday, and a pretty important one at that. For the eleventh time that morning, Mom was climbing the stairs to the second floor of what some snoopy realtor once referred to as our "upscale suburban home" in Encino, CA. Ed must've had enough cardio for the day because I could hear him snoring peacefully somewhere near my bed. As Mom marched into my room, I braced myself. She was about to resume what the Navarro clan likes to call—Dunt-Dunt-DUN—The Beggar's Sideshow.

So, all you derps out there who are heavy sleepers, you'll get where I'm coming from. The Beggar's Sideshow, which was shorthand for "How to Get Ruby Out of Bed Without Losing My Freaking Mind," was a masterwork of music, yodeling, and found art that had been honed to perfection over a period of, well, fourteen years. It required, among other things, several large clocks of both the battery-powered and wind-up variety (each with an ear-splitting alarm), a creepy clown doll named Mr. Shivers (purchased at a yard sale when I was three that bore a striking resemblance to Johnny Depp in a blood-stained party dress and mysteriously repeated the phrase *Nuts to you, Wes!* in a Swiss accent whenever you pulled its string), an iPhone-Bluetooth speaker combo with the volume turned way up, and wait for it...

A cowbell.

You heard me right. I think Mom believed the cowbell was a stroke of genius because she was very fond of it. She had purchased it, as well as a cowbell beater, at a local music store owned by a nice family from Minnesota by the name of Swensen. When my mother first told this story, I lost it.

Apparently, the pimply-faced kid who sold her the items had made an awkward pass. He, in fact, had said to her—and I quote—"Want me to come over later and show you how to use those?" Oh my gosh, *so* Chad Radwell!

Fortunately, the store manager overheard the horny little dweeb and said, "I told you boyce about talkin' to the customers. Go checksie da toilet and give it a good scrub."

Reportedly, "Chad" made a frowny face. "What, now?"

"Yup." The manager turned to my mother and said, "Sorry. You gotta stay on 'em. Give me a jingle if you got any questions."

Like a scene out of *Fargo*, am I right? Yer dern-tootin'!

Anyways. I was lying in bed, fully awake, thanks to some thoughtless jerk outside who felt it was a good time to fire up a chainsaw. But I will admit, I do possess a bit of an evil streak and wanted to catch Mom's performance. So, I played dead. Standing just out of my reach, she raised the cowbell beater and launched into "Honky Tonk Women." Usually I let her get about eight bars in before cracking an eye open.

"I'm awake," I said, trying to sound all Liv Moore on depressed teenager brain.

"Sure you don't want to hear my solo? I've been practicing."

At this point, I was pretty much done. "Can you please stop?"

"Come on, one chorus."

"No-uh!"

And that, friends and neighbors, is The Beggar's Sideshow. Tah-dah!

～

BREAKFAST WAS BETTER. Once I get some food in me, I am actually quite pleasant. At this point, you're probably wondering what I look like—the whole "Ruby vibe" and all. Well, I'm slightly below average in height. Mom says I might hit a growth spurt when I'm a junior. I have straight, shoulder-length blonde hair (courtesy of my mother), which I tend to keep in a ponytail, brown eyes (my father's), and dimples, which only ever make an appearance when I'm tickled (which *no one* is allowed to do, by the way—not even my posse). My shoes consist mostly of high-top Converse sneakers in various shades. I tend to wear out the red ones. And my body, well... That's my business.

"Mom?" I said, my mouth full of half-burnt raisin toast piled high with Philadelphia whipped cream cheese and dripping with Seville orange marmalade, which we'd recently purchased at Monsieur Marcel in Farmers Market.

"Yeah?"

My mother was already dressed for work—I am totally stealing that Lavish Alice cape blazer—but had called in to say she would be coming in late. This was a big day for her, too.

"What time is Dad coming?"

She didn't wear a watch and was always scrambling to find her phone whenever anyone asked her for the time.

"Any minute," she said.

"Yikes, I haven't even showered yet!"

Oh, that's another one of my sterling qualities. I have zero ability to manage my schedule.

Smiling, Mom watched as I burst out of my chair and raced up the stairs, practically tripping over the dog, who had absolutely no business curling up on the bottom step. Fifteen minutes later, I was running back down, fully dressed and schlepping a camo Army duffel bag I found on sale at Wasteland.

"Is he here yet?" I said, out of breath.

"Not yet. Did you remember to brush your teeth?"

I practically raced to the foyer and deposited the duffel bag next to the front door when my phone went into the *Poltergeist* theme song. Groaning (I'm a groaner from way back), I pulled it out of my back pocket, saw it was Diego, and quickly texted, *Can't talk*. He replied, *Nos vemos*, followed by a little taco emoji. I was pounding out, *Later, dude*, followed by a series of inspired emojis, when I heard my mother's voice from the kitchen and instantly rolled my eyes, since it is a scientific fact the two are darkly connected, like barnacle geese and goose barnacles. Look it up.

"Last chance, Ruby," Mom said.

I heard a light tapping on the cowbell and knew what was coming next. In fact, I lip-synced the words as they left her lips.

"Are you absolutely sure you want to do this?"

And there it was. Mom guilt in all its West Coast suburban glory. Where was Dad already? I needed to blow this pop stand.

"Mom, please, not again."

She emerged from the kitchen, holding my extra one-terabyte hard drive. It's funny. As mad as I get at Mom sometimes, I do love looking at her face. She's beautiful, with these soft blue-green eyes I wish I had. Only, over time they had sort of congealed with fatalism and worry. Is this what it meant to be an adult? Sign me up.

"Thanks," I said.

I reached for the device and tossed it into the duffel bag, where I discovered Mr. Shivers hiding in my underwear. I grabbed the doll and turned to Mom.

"Hey, don't look at me," she said.

I opened the foyer closet door and threw the doll in. Mom was on her knees, closing my duffel bag for me. I realized she was working extra hard at being mature, but it was pretty obvious she was worried about her only daughter. She was probably asking herself why she'd even agreed to this nutty arrangement. Actually, I was surprised myself.

My phone buzzed again. This time it was Claire. *Not now*, I quickly texted back. She responded with a sad face emoji.

"What if he doesn't look after you properly?"

Mom was picking lint off her skirt, which unfortunately was a nervous habit I picked up.

"Mom, I'll be okay. It's not like he's some pervy relative—"

"Ruby, where did you—"

The doorbell rang—saved!—but it set the dog off. Honestly, when it comes to doorbells, nothing beats a Shih Tzu. Ed bolted between my legs, almost causing me to trip, so he could get to the door first.

"Ed!"

It was Dad, of course.

I don't know why, but suddenly, I let out this weird little laugh, sort of like that possessed deer head in *Evil Dead II*. In my defense, I hadn't seen him since the 13 Frightened Girls concert, which he'd taken me to as a surprise, even though he himself prefers straight-ahead jazz. He always looks so impressive, too. I mean, not being a very straight-laced gal, I could still appreciate the sharp gray suit and slightly long dark brown hair. And he's tall—I like that. When he walked through the door, I noticed he was still wearing his wedding ring.

"Hey, baby. You ready?" he said.

I was practically blinded by the million-dollar smile that had somehow survived the breakup. Even the dog was taken in, rolling onto his back and waiting for a belly rub.

Time to play it cool.

"Could you get that bag?" I said. "It's really heavy."

But Dad wasn't paying attention. No, he was looking at Mom. And it was awkward because I'm pretty sure he was still in love with her.

"Hi, Stace," he said. "You're looking good."

"You, too."

She pretended to search for something in her purse. Wow, could it be she loved him, too?

"Dad, the bag?" I said, trying to break the tension.

He grabbed the duffel bag, and, like an old man getting up from the table at Hometown Buffet, he staggered out the door, muttering. Yeah, despite all his excellent qualities, my dad's a mutterer.

"And make sure he keeps food in the house," Mom said with a fatalism Anna Karenina would admire.

She slipped me a paper bag that was warm and smelled good. Unbelievable. Though she had been married to the man for fifteen years, she genuinely worried he would forget to feed me.

I touched her arm and gave her my most serious expression. "Everything will be fine."

"*I'm* supposed to say that."

As Dad jogged back inside, Mom hugged me deeply, as if she were never going to see me again. But I knew it would be okay, even though the thought of being away for the whole summer reminded me of how much we as a family had lost in the past year. It was unnatural and happened every day.

Ed was being annoying, sitting at my feet and whining

softly. Feeling sorry for him, I knelt and waited for him to roll over so I could scratch his belly.

"Who's going to miss me?" I said. "Who's going to miss me bad? *You* are!" Then to Mom, "Can't I take Ed with me?"

She scrunched her face and looked at Dad. "It's up to your father."

"Dad, pleeeeeeze?"

"Fine, but *you're* walking him," he said.

"Yay!"

I ran into the kitchen and returned with the dog's food, bowls, and leash.

"Don't forget to call," Mom said, her voice wavering. Next up, the waterworks. It was definitely time to jet.

"Mom, we gotta go."

I quickly headed out with Dad and Ed as Mom watched, biting her lower lip. Yeah, she's a lip-biter. Wow, three months. How would she survive without her baby? One time while sleuthing, I ran across this old video from when I was practically brand new. Dad had been recording me as I lay in my crib. He loves making home movies; we have tons. Anyways, the two of them were talking.

"Is day care really the best thing for her?" Mom said as she tightened the sheet over the mattress and checked my sleeper.

"Come on, Stace," Dad said off-camera.

I could tell they had done this bit a million times before because it sounded rehearsed.

"What better security can she have than two working parents? My mom—"

"Worked her whole life and managed to raise a wonderful son." She made a face. "Alan, I know. But something in me—"

"Everything will be fine," he said.

"Promise?"

Unfortunately, the tape ended there, so we'll never know if he had actually promised her. I wondered which part of me Mom would get to keep and which was going with her soon-to-be ex-husband once the divorce was final. You know, that would make for an interesting science experiment. LOL.

3

"How many times do we have to go through this, Son? Your grandmother is *dead!*"

— PARANORMAN

Don't get me wrong. I was psyched to be spending the entire summer with my dad. I loved Mom, but enough was enough. I needed to hang out with the Big Guy for a while. That was not to say Dad didn't have his own issues. Currently, number one on his hit parade was a certain Stacey Navarro. I was going to have to play this very carefully. I didn't want to give away too much info, but I also didn't want to blow him off. He would totally see through that. Hmm, or would he? Mom once told me men were thick. Nevertheless, I thought it better not to take any chances.

We were weaving through midday traffic on the 405 in Dad's new Lexus NX Hybrid. Ed was safely harnessed in the backseat. I had on my Wayfarers and, as we passed the Getty Center, I noticed some preppy from Harvard-Westlake oh-so-casually checking me out as he sped by us in his Porsche. *Be cool, Ruby!* I loved that Dad worked at a car dealership. We got to tool around in these fantastic late-model vehicles and pretend we were somebody. For all this bub knew, I was on my way to the *American Horror Story* set to do a walk-on with Billie Lourd.

I grabbed a snickerdoodle from the paper bag Mom had given me, checked on Ed, and fiddled with the GPS. Dad was too distracted to notice. Probably because he'd been looking forward to this day for weeks and, now that it was here, he didn't know what to say. Typical male of the species. Look, I knew Dad loved me and all, but lately he seemed more like a stranger. And he was. Living apart from Mom and me had really hurt our relationship. Time to break the ice.

"I can't wait for self-driving cars," I said, keeping my eyes on the road.

"What? Hey, don't break that!"

Gently, he pulled my hand away from the controls and looked at me with these huge, sincere puppy-dog eyes. Oh, boy. I'd hoped to keep things light, but I could tell my father was in a rut and wanted to spill about the thing that was bothering him. I should've picked up on the clues—the nervous finger-tapping and the random humming—and misdirected him with a quick chorus of "Just A Girl." But it was too late. Before I could open my mouth, Dad stepped in it with both feet.

"So, does she talk about me?" he said.

I could feel my mouth going lopsided, which apparently is a thing I do whenever I'm confronted with the kind of bald-faced idiocy only a man could muster. I coughed, spraying cookie crumbs on the car's nice clean interior.

"Dad!" I said.

He turned to me, looking confused. "What, honey? Are those snickerdoodles?"

Hmm, so we were playing hardball.

"She doesn't say anything. She's, I don't know, getting on with her life?"

"I see."

Do you remember Carl at the beginning of Season 4 of *The Walking Dead*, when Farmer Rick no longer permitted him to carry a weapon? That's what Dad looked like. Not even an hour into my vacation, and summer already sucked. Nice going, Alan.

"And we're not doing this third degree all summer," I said. "It's boring."

"Sure, no problem."

I might have gone a bit too far, having accused my own dear father of being the B-word. *Boring.* Like our neighbor Boyd, who taught geometry at a nearby charter school, drove a Corolla, ate SunChips, and was a champion thumb wrestler. Boyd, who liked to use words like "discombobulated," "sammich," "back atcha," and "yea big." Boyd, who was happily married to an equally boring woman named Barbara, had four healthy young children —whose names all began with B—and a twenty-year mortgage. Boyd, who took the family on annual driving vacations to visit relatives in Nebraska. Great. Now I felt awful.

Dad let me stew in my own juices for a while. Eventually, we exited at Santa Monica Boulevard.

"Want a burger?" he said.

It was like nothing had happened. Hmm... I think Mom may have underestimated men. Not that *I'm* thick! I totally saw what he was doing, but here's the thing, I couldn't turn down a burger. No way. Already imagining the succulent juices dribbling down my chin, I found myself laughing like the little girl he no doubt remembered. Oh, he was good.

"Can we go to Shake Shack?" I said.

"I don't know."

"Pleeeeeeze?"

"That place is always too crowded. Let's try Irv's."

"Fine," I said. "By the way, this wouldn't be a bribe, would it?"

"Hey, would I bribe my own daughter?"

Can I get an amen?

IF HORROR IS MY LIFE, then meat is my passion. Beef, especially. So when Dad suggested a hamburger, you can see why I folded like a $5.99 camping chair from Walmart. Anyways. The traffic at Santa Monica and Laurel was nonstop and the parking nonexistent as we pulled up to the venerable Irv's Burgers in West Hollywood. Fun fact for ya —Jim Morrison and Janis Joplin used to hang out there. Well, at the old location. Mom said they were famous musicians.

Eventually, we found a parking spot several blocks away and were now sitting at a small outdoor table, eating cheeseburgers. The great thing about Irv's is, it doesn't matter how you are dressed or where you're from or how old you are. We were like a family. One large, carnivorous family.

"I love burgers, don't you?" I said, my mouth shiny with meat juice.

Dad was still distracted. "Yeah, I do. Listen—"

"I'm pretty sure I was a cannibal in a former life."

"A cannibal?"

"Did you know scientists have learned that cannibalism goes back at least fifty-thousand years?"

Hoping to avoid any mention of Mom, I continued the anthropology lesson, but my father was finding it harder and harder to stay focused. Look, he's really a very sweet guy —the best. And I'll bet he had intended to keep all this Stacey business to himself. But from the way he was looking at me, like I might be the NSA of Mom-tel, I knew he was going to pump me for information, or explode.

"Has Mom mentioned any male that's not me?" Dad said, not making direct eye contact.

Though I felt sorry for the guy, I rolled my eyes and flung an angry fry at his head. It bounced and landed on the sidewalk, only to be inhaled instantly by Ed.

"I'm going to eat *you*, if you don't quit it!"

To my surprise, he changed the subject.

"Listen, Rube," he said. "Before we go to the apartment, I need to stop off at the dealership. Hope you don't mind."

"Sure, no prob."

"Great. Are you done?"

"Hang on!"

Now, I am proud to say I'm a total vacuum cleaner when it comes to food. But as good as I am, I needed more than a few seconds to make half a cheeseburger, a basket of fries drenched in ketchup, and a large Diet Coke disappear. In the end, I beat my old record and came in at a minute-forty-five. In your face, Slimer!

IT TOOK us twenty minutes to get to the West Side. Dad worked at Lexus of Santa Monica and had been their top performer for, like, forever. Nevertheless, he hated the sales manager, Rick Van Loon. Though he had never put it into words, I could always tell there was this tension whenever those two were in the same room together. Sort of like Sam and Dean confronting Crowley.

"Wait here in the showroom and look at cars or something," Dad said, handing me a brochure. "I need to see Rick."

"Sure, Daddy-O."

"And don't ever call me that."

"Roger that."

Dad abandoned me, so to pass the time, I Snapchatted with Claire and Diego. Presently, I was sending them pics of Ed and me mugging inside the new cars while Claire gave us a quick clarinet concert and Diego showed me what it was like hanging curtains with his mom. When I turned around, I could see my father through the glass of Rick's office, fidgeting and looking around.

Rick was standing in front of the big board, pointing at the names of the salespeople and their ranking. Dad's name was at the very top, of course. I decided to eavesdrop and, putting away my phone, positioned Ed and myself outside Rick's office, out of sight.

It was pretty obvious to me why Dad hated this guy. He was making these annoying clicking noises with his tongue as he used a dry-erase marker to update the numbers. Truly, he was a strange, grubby little poser who, despite his position, liked wearing ill-fitting Macy's suits, and he had dandruff and smelled like Dentyne. On his desk sat a framed photo of himself with the governor. Photoshop, most likely.

Oh, and there was something else about Rick you should know. He was pretty much a washout with the ladies. I didn't know if he insulted them or what. But he must've done something bad recently because one of his eyes was swollen shut and two fingers were taped together.

"Hot date last night, Rick?" Dad said.

Though Rick's legendary facial tic was kicking in, he refused to take the bait.

"So! Looks like you're a shoo-in to win the sales contest this month."

Way to go, Dad! You know, I think my evil streak might have come from him. I could see he wasn't letting this go. Smiling, he continued to poke the bear.

"Are you going to press charges this time?"

Rick's cheeks got tight and the pupil in his good eye became a pinpoint. It was as if his entire face was controlled by a single wire that Dad was gleefully manipulating.

"My personal life is not up for discussion."

Rick had said this with an air of importance only a short man could pull off. Boy, Dad must've gotten to him because the next thing Rick did was accidentally knock the photo to the floor, sending glass everywhere. As Dad helpfully picked up the frame, he noticed something. Now I saw it, too—it was the corner of another photo behind the first. *What the...*

Before Dad could say anything, Rick grabbed the broken frame and shoved it into a desk drawer.

"Thank you!" he said.

His face was three shades of red. Popping a couple of fresh sticks of Dentyne into his pie hole, he sat back and smiled like Dexter.

"Hey, are you and Stacey still trying to—"

Wait, did he just mention my mother? When the receptionist Gina came over, I ducked out fast, dragging Ed behind me.

Gina Wallace was a nice girl with unusually large eyes, a cute figure, and these tiny little teeth that reminded me of Del

Monte white corn. Whenever I saw her, I got the feeling she was waiting for Rick to "come to his senses" and pick *her*, instead of going another round with the Ronda Rouseys of the world. Thanks to Dad, I knew Gina's whole sordid history. Over the years, she'd nursed Rick through cracked ribs, broken toes, damaged kidneys, and a singed uvula, which happened the time he went out with a fire eater from a Polish circus.

"Alan, Ms. Heatherly is here," Gina said, pretending not to notice Rick.

"I thought I was seeing her tomorrow. Okay, thanks, Gina." Dad smirked at Rick. "Are we done here?"

"Sure, sure," Rick said. "Mr. Contest Winner." Then to Gina, "Can you get someone in here to clean up this glass?"

Rick always said "someone" when everyone, including the Pope, knew he meant Gina. And that poor girl would always pretend to call the maintenance guy, when I'd bet a dollar in five minutes she would be back with a broom and dustpan. Sad, really, when you think about it.

As Dad strolled into the showroom, Gina and I watched as an attractive woman wearing Armani checked out one of the new models. Gina tugged on Dad's coat sleeve.

"Elizabeth Banks?" she said.

"Ooh, close."

Adjusting his tie, he sauntered over to the woman, wearing that million-dollar smile. It was on.

"Ms. Heatherly! Alan Navarro. You know, you remind me of Charlize Theron."

One of these days I was going to figure out how he did that. And I was about to say this to Gina when I noticed she was gone. A minute later I saw her walking into Rick's office, carrying—you guessed it—a broom and dustpan. Easy money.

I HATED Dad living away from us, but at least he had a nice apartment off Sunset in West Hollywood. Relatively new and smelling faintly of paint, it had three bedrooms, one of which Dad used as his home office. He had done his best to make my room comfortable but, let's face it, he was a guy, so. Though he had moved in a year ago, all I could see were stacks of moving boxes. Rather than deal with it, I shooed him out. I would have to make the best of things and live out of my duffel bag like a hobo.

After a dinner of spicy beef and Jasmine rice from the Vietnamese place around the corner, I sat at a small desk with my laptop, working away at my beloved machinima project while Ed lay on the floor, snoring. Other than horror, machinima was the best thing ever. Using a variety of software programs, I could create my own movies, populated by ghosts, demons, and evil clowns. Someday, I hoped to start my own video game company. Or I might write and direct movies. That would be cool, too.

This latest project was about a crazed killer. He didn't have a name yet, but he wore the black hat and duster I designed. I had been having trouble with his chainsaw when I happened to connect with a software developer in Norway who liked to create cool weapons. I was able to import a lumberjack special that looked amazing. This guy even provided the audio for it.

A loud yawn startled me. It was Dad. *How long had he been standing there?*

"Come on, Rube, it's late," he said.

And by the way, when did he get all parental? Mom must've had a talk with him.

"No-uh," I said. "I need to figure out this sequence." Between you and me, I was struggling to keep my eyes open.

Gently, he closed the laptop and guided me to my bed. As I dug through the duffel bag for my pajamas, I felt something foreign. Removing my hand, I saw Mr. Shivers. *How had he gotten in there again?* I thought I'd left him in the closet back home. Too exhausted to care, I tossed him into a chair, where he landed in a sitting position.

"Tomorrow, I could use your help setting up the Roku," Dad said.

"Aghh, you're so pathetic. Fine, I'll see what I can do."

I let go of a major yawn. Smiling, he gave me a bear hug, practically squeezing the air out of me.

"Ooh, I thought I heard a fart."

"Dad, that's so rude!"

"It used to make you laugh."

"When I was five."

"Good night, Rube. Brush your teeth."

He and Mom had definitely spoken. I wondered vaguely if he was going to go off and practice The Beggar's Sideshow per Mom's instructions. Before he left, I broke down and decided to spill. After all, the man deserved to know the truth. I picked Ed up and put him on my lap for moral support.

"Dad?"

"Yeah, baby?"

"She *is* moving on, you know."

He was leaning against the doorframe, staring at me intently. I could almost see the man hormones keeping his emotions in check. Barely. His face was a mosaic of disappointment, anger, and disbelief. He smiled sadly and, without another word, closed the door behind him. See, this is the difference between women and men. I would be throwing things at this point.

Lying in bed, I tossed around like that stupid paper boat in *It*. I glanced at my phone to see the time. It was late. Ed was sitting on the floor motionless, looking at something. I followed his gaze. Across from me on the chair, Mr. Shivers sat staring at me, his eyes flat. I looked away and happened to notice the ceiling. A strange-looking stain was taking shape. It was blob-like and creepy. I hoped a pipe hadn't sprung a leak.

"Nuts to you, Wes," the doll said.

It took me a few minutes to calm down. As I closed my eyes, I pondered men versus women, crazed killers with chainsaws, and a plate of beef medallions I once enjoyed at a swanky hotel in San Francisco. Only now they were screaming like Mandrakes as I sliced into them with my gleaming steak knife.

4

"Out of all the women in the whole world, he chose you."

— ROSEMARY'S BABY

I t was hot in downtown LA—ghost peppers in a grease fire hot. In the distance, lines of cars clogged the swollen arteries of the Harbor Freeway. A solitary *paletero* with one leg shorter than the other was crossing the bridge at 3rd Street, the little bell on his cart tinkling merrily with the promise of delicious fresh-fruit ices.

Eventually, he passed a tall, pretty redhead in a black cocktail dress, walking in the opposite direction. Her name was Laraine Moody, and the Mexican vendor could tell she'd been crying. When he saw the bruises on her pale, freckled arms, he knew what Ana Gabriel was talking about when she sang "Y Aquí Estoy."

Through his large office window in the tallest building in LA, Warren Mudge peered through Nikon ProStaff binoculars and caught sight of the *paletero* as he vanished around a corner. Wiping a hungered droplet of drool from his lip, he realized he would have to hunt the old dude down later. The Chief Marketing Officer of Viper Leather Goods, Warren was in his mid-fifties and had a weakness for *paletas*—especially the *pepino con chile y limón*.

Though he was short, he did not suffer from achondroplasia. On the contrary, his body was proportional and muscled. He kept himself in shape by running, swimming, and climbing, and he adhered to a strict paleo diet—except for the *paletas*—while eschewing cigarettes and alcohol. Also, Warren was a skydiving freak and liked to escape to Elsinore Valley whenever he could.

As he leaned back comfortably at his luxurious antique walnut desk, Stacey Navarro knocked and came in, taking a seat opposite her boss. She noticed the newly framed photos of Warren's most recent skydiving exploits hanging on the wall. She'd been meaning to tell him she had never been skydiving in her life and had no intention of starting, but now was not the time.

"Stacey, the marketing campaign is fantastic," he said, waving his arms like he was giving a TED Talk. "So far, the UK, Benelux, and Saudi Arabia are seeing results."

"Well, I learned from the best." Stacey was nothing if not modest.

"Hmm... A man would've taken credit."

"I know, Warren, but—"

"Close the door."

She knew what was coming. And she wanted it, but at the same time, she didn't. In the eighteen months she'd worked at Viper, Warren had promoted her twice and given her generous bonuses. He had always treated her with respect and courtesy. But after the separation, things had progressed to a new, almost uncomfortable level. Was she ready for this?

"Stacey, have you thought any more about the offer?"

The offer. He made it sound like he was buying an investment property in Montana. She looked at him, her eyes distant. In her mind, she pictured the wedding photo of Alan and her, which used to sit on the mantle, going up in flames. *Please stop,* she thought as he slid a handcrafted rosewood ring box across the desk toward her. *Please, can you go back to being my boss?*

For a long time, she stared at the box with the tasteful scrollwork. Somewhere far off, a lunatic had fired up a chainsaw, its angry whine echoing just outside the window, even though they were on a high floor. She reached for the present with trembling fingers. Opening it, she beheld a huge diamond engagement ring.

"Oh my," she said.

That's when things changed. Warren was no longer wearing a suit. He had on casual clothes, the kind you'd find at Barneys New York. The skydiving photos were gone, replaced by family portraits. Stacey saw herself holding a newborn baby and posing next to Warren. Ruby was standing on her other side, and everyone was smiling. Outside, it was raining.

"I don't want us to wait any longer," he said from somewhere far away. "How soon can you make the divorce final?"

But Stacey could only sit there, as frozen as the precious gem in front of her.

It was the dwarf's fault. Alan knew it in his soul. The homunculus in question was, of course, Warren Nathaniel Mudge. *Mudge.* It sounded like something that would clog your pipes, if you weren't careful. Also, it rhymed with grudge. Which was perfect because now that Alan thought about it, he did have one nasty grudge against that evil mastermind. In fact, he would like to rip Mudge's testicles off and feed them to one of Rick Van Loon's feral dates. It was because of that smirking, hunchbacked miscreant that Alan would lose the one great love of his life. That hirsute, grinning, piston-headed—

"Alan, are you even listening?"

He looked up from his half-eaten marinated skirt steak frites and stared cloudily into Stacey's eyes. Those eyes. Perfectly blue with flecks of green. He adored those eyes. In fact, he had fallen in love with Stacey because of those eyes. That and so many other things.

When his hearing returned, he noticed the BOA Steakhouse was unusually loud, as if each table were in a cheerleading competition at a Toastmasters convention. It was lunchtime, and the place was packed, both at the tables and the bar. Runners with trays of food scurried past in a dizzy dance. Somewhere a glass shattered.

"I'm sorry," he said. "I don't think I—"

"I said, Warren has asked me to marry him."

"But we're not even divorced!" The color had left his face. "And since when is he in the picture?"

"Keep your voice down." Stacey, sounding as if she were addressing a misbehaving child, caught herself and softened her tone. "Obviously, this is going to take some time to figure out."

Alan tasted vomit as he tried reasoning with her. "Hey, come on," he said, putting on the million-dollar smile. "The guy's been married—"

"Twice. I know. But he's older now, more mature. He's a decent man."

"Decent?"

"He wants a family."

"So did Charles Manson. And look how that turned out. Besides, you *have* a family."

"He wants me to quit my job and stay home."

"I see what this is about. You think our marriage was a mistake."

"I didn't say that."

"And I'm a schmuck because I believe everyone needs to work."

"Alan..."

As a dessert tray flew by, he snatched a slice of mascarpone cheesecake, scraped off a glob of vanilla Chantilly cream with his forefinger, and deposited it on Stacey's steak.

She stared at him, uncomprehending. "What's this for?"

"It's the icing on the steak."

Immediately regretting what he'd done, he got up and threw down some cash on the table.

"You're being unfair," she said, her voice like shards of ice.

"*I'm* being unfair?" Straightening his tie, he glanced around the room, then leaned in toward his wife. "I thought we had a shot. I guess I'm having a harder time 'moving on.'"

"What? Alan, this isn't a contest."

He recognized the weariness in her voice. It was the same weariness he had picked up on when they were first having their difficulties a year ago. *Had it been a year already? Ruby was fourteen!* He took a last look at his soon-to-be ex-wife and walked out, muttering. Then, he remembered he didn't have any cash for the valet.

Staring at the sugary white topping melting on her steak, Stacey felt frustrated and alone. She wanted to scream and suddenly hated the hairpiece of the man sitting across from her. It wasn't supposed to go this way. Why couldn't people be civilized?

A memory came flooding back to her of a night eleven years earlier when she and Alan were lying in bed. Long before iPads had been invented, they'd settled the problem of what to watch by setting up two televisions side-by-side at the foot of the bed. She remembered he was watching *The Apartment*. She was multitasking, reading a book on infertility and half-watching the original *A Nightmare on Elm Street*—one of her favorites because it featured Johnny Depp in his pre-Jack Sparrow days.

"I heard something," she said, yanking off her headphones.

Still wearing his, Alan sat in bed, engrossed in the scene where Jack Lemmon finds Shirley MacLaine lying on his bed, unconscious from an overdose of sleeping pills. With mother determination, she got out of bed and rushed to Ruby's bedroom. When she didn't see her daughter, her heart skipped a beat. As she made her way down the stairs, she heard giggling coming from the home office. Rushing in, she found Ruby, three at the time, playing a computer game.

"Ruby, why aren't you in bed?"

As Alan walked in, he yawned loudly. "What's going on?"

Stacey glared at him, angry at his seeming lack of concern. "Your daughter is playing *Warcraft: Orcs & Humans* again."

"Look, Daddy!" Ruby said, pointing proudly at the monitor.

"Are you kidding me?" He came over and squinted at the screen. "How did you manage to kill all those orcs?"

Stacey rolled her eyes. "Alan, that's not really the point."

"I know, but—"

"Back to bed, Ruby. *Now!*" Stacey was pointing at the door.

"Come on, short stack," Alan said, picking up his daughter and depositing her on his shoulders.

"Whee!"

Back in bed, Alan reached over to turn out the light, but Stacey set her book down and grabbed his arm.

"Ow! Look, it's not my fault she keeps guessing my password," he said.

"Let's make a baby."

"Now? What about the schedule?"

Smiling, she climbed onto him and, switching off the light, kissed him. "Schedule, shmedule."

Sitting glumly at her table at the BOA Steakhouse, Stacey could still feel that kiss, as well as a profound sadness. She would marry Warren, and Alan would find someone. They would have joint custody of Ruby. She and Warren would have children of their own, and so would Alan and whoever he wound up with—probably someone younger who attended barre classes. Everyone would get together on holidays, and Ruby would be well adjusted.

Why was she having so much trouble picturing Alan with someone else? *Come on, Stacey, think.* All those women who came into the dealership every day? She was perfectly aware they found him attractive. As she had. Short blondes with big breasts, tall brunettes with legs up to their eyeballs. Oddly, no redheads. *Everything will be fine,* she told herself. Alan would eventually meet someone. The important thing for him was to get back out there.

Still, was that the future she wanted? This wasn't one of her promotions. Warren had proposed, for God's sake. And another thing. Why had she been in such a hurry to tell Alan? To hurt him? Yes—*no!* The truth was, she *had* hurt him. Deeply. Surprisingly, it hadn't been that hard to do. In fact, it had felt...*good.*

As Stacey looked down at her cold plate, she watched in silent dread as fresh blood oozed from underneath the meat, as if something precious had just been sacrificed.

"God, I love you."

— MISERY

Alan sat at his computer, poring over videos of his wedding: Stacey getting ready with the help of her mother and her friends, the wedding party posing outside the Catholic church in Brentwood, and Alan's mother sitting alone at the reception while his father, stepmother, and half-brother, Matt, sat uncomfortably at a different table. Matt had worn a black Homburg for the occasion.

Like the rest of his apartment, Alan's office was a clutter of moving boxes, old magazines, and video cassettes. Though he had bought new furniture and accessories for every room, he had never had the energy to clean up the mess. As he slumped in his chair, his head throbbed and he thought he tasted blood. No wonder. He had bitten the inside of his cheek again.

This routine had become a habit, spending his nights

sifting through old home movies. At first, he had simply wanted to relive the happiness of his marriage to Stacey, followed by an idyllic life with their daughter. But as he dug deeper and realized how much footage he had accumulated over the years, a vague idea began to take form—that he could somehow pull together years of memories into a single, cohesive narrative that would prove to Stacey how much they had meant to each other and what a tragedy it would be if they divorced.

But that was as far as he had gotten.

From a practical perspective, he was talking hundreds of hours of video. No one—not even Stacey—would sit through that. He needed to find the best parts and string them together—a "sizzle reel." And he needed music. It was all so confusing. Usually, he would become depressed, crack open a beer, and put on *An Affair to Remember* or *Roman Holiday*, depending on how many tissue boxes he planned to go through.

Alan stared at the monitor grimly, images of Stacey in her wedding dress dancing in front of him. She was radiant. His eyes moist, he watched her longingly and wondered again, as he had so many other nights, what on God's green earth had happened to them. Getting up and stretching, he rubbed his red eyes and went to check on Ruby.

She was asleep at her laptop, still wearing her earbuds. The small flat screen TV was on—*Halloween: The Curse of Michael Myers*. How could she watch that stuff? Why not *Jersey Girl* or *13 Going on 30*? He leaned over to close Ruby's laptop. The screen was frozen on a scene from her machinima project. Alan cringed.

The image was striking. A man who looked very much like him was on his knees, his head and arms raised in supplication to a dark, boiling sky. A chill went through him. *Not healthy*, he thought as he snapped the laptop cover shut.

The dog was asleep on the bed. As quietly as possible, he picked Ed up and transferred him to the floor. Gently, he removed Ruby's earbuds and thought he heard the tail end of "New Slang." He carried her to the bed and turned off the TV. He was surprised at how light she was. She groaned softly as he lay her head on the pillow. He stood gazing at her slender wrists and long, delicate fingers. Then, he drew the duvet over her. No matter what happened, she would always be his little girl.

Lying in bed, Alan tried to sleep, but it was useless. He wanted to get out of the apartment for a while, so he checked his watch. He hoped Mrs. Tessenbaum was awake.

CATALINA'S WASN'T CROWDED. The small jazz club on Sunset was a favorite hangout of Alan's. He liked it because it was more intimate than places like Vibrato Grill, though the décor wasn't much to speak of. A jazz quartet was playing onstage when he walked in. He headed straight for the bar and ordered an IPA.

"I had this dream," he said.

He liked telling his dreams to the pretty bartender because she was married, which meant she was safe, at least to his way of thinking.

"I'm in this very ornate room. I think it's French Baroque. And in the center is a Louis XIV table with a big pink donut box sitting on top. I can almost smell the donuts. But when I open the box, I find stacks of rare books containing some of the greatest knowledge of the universe."

The bartender played along. "And do you open the books?"

"No. Right when I'm about to, I wake up." He took another swallow of beer. "The thing is, I was really craving a donut after that."

"Huh," she said as she placed a fresh beer next to the one on the bar.

"You have to tell me what it means."

"Maybe you think you want these rare, beautiful things most people never even think about. But in the end, what you want is what everyone wants."

"A donut?"

She gave him the high sign. He turned around to find a tall, attractive redhead wearing a red cocktail dress. It was Laraine Moody. Her hair and lips were full, and her jewelry glinted in the lights from the stage. Raising the new beer to her, he smiled weakly. She winked.

"You're not gonna try your line out on her?" the bartender said.

"What line is that?"

"'You remind me of Corpse Bride. Only prettier.'"

"You know me too well, kid."

Eventually, Laraine stepped up to the microphone as the band broke into "You'd Be So Nice To Come Home To." Her voice was low and smoky, which Alan found intriguing. She sang directly to him, and he pretended he didn't notice. With the exception of Marilyn Monroe to President Kennedy, men didn't like to be sung to.

He buried his face in his hands. Others were looking at him now, wondering what the connection was. His heart started to race, and he wished there was a fire alarm he could set off. When she wouldn't stop, he dug out some cash, tossed it on the bar, and walked out as the music swelled.

ALAN HANDED a twenty to Mrs. Tessenbaum, his elderly next-door neighbor. As a young girl, she had been rescued by the Americans from Dachau in the spring of 1945, along with her older brother and an uncle. Though she had lived through that hell, she had grown up to be a cheerful woman with a German accent who loved her dog and always referred to her late husband as "Mr. Tessenbaum."

"Thanks again for watching her, Mrs. T.," he said, opening the front door for her.

"It's no trouble, you know that." She clucked her tongue disapprovingly. "You're too young to be sad, Alan."

"I know. Have you ever dreamt about donuts?"

"Ruby is such a cute girl. And your wife, Stacey. *Oy!* Such a beauty, that one."

"Who's about to marry Rumpelstiltskin. She doesn't love me."

He was surprised he had said it out loud. But it needed to be said. It was what he'd been feeling since that disastrous lunch the other day. The truth was, Stacey no longer loved him and was moving on. Soon, he would be utterly alone.

"So much you don't understand," the old woman said as they stood in the hallway. She smiled at his confused expression. "Women don't fall out of love, Alan. It's taken from us."

She kissed him tenderly on the cheek and headed back to her apartment. "Good night, *boychik*," she said over her shoulder.

"Good night, Mrs. T."

Later, sipping a steaming cup of coffee at his computer, Alan resumed editing his home movies because he wasn't going down without a fight. Warren Mudge was an orc, and orcs could be defeated. Yawning, he glanced at his watch. One-thirty. Plenty of time. They would see.

He was creating a masterpiece.

6

"Help! Someone help me! Is someone there? Hey! Shit, I'm probably dead."

— Saw

An annoying tapping noise woke me from an epic snore-a-thon, so no need for The Beggar's Sideshow today. Why was I dressed? I didn't remember falling asleep. And had Dad gone out? Vague flashes danced in my head. One of them was of the old Jewish lady from next door sticking her head in and whispering something in Yiddish. Yawning, I sat up and noticed a song sparrow pecking at my window. Well, that explained the tapping.

"Shoo!" I said, flinging a blue decorative pillow at the bird. "I hope Dad remembered the Froot Loops," I said to Mr. Shivers.

After walking Ed, I checked the kitchen. Dad was nowhere in sight. I looked at the time on my phone. It was past eight. The dealership didn't open until nine. Shouldn't he be in the kitchen, making us breakfast? I checked his bedroom. Huh. The bed was made up. Could he have left already?

I tried the home office and discovered my father with his head on the computer keyboard, wheezing like a walrus who'd swallowed another walrus. On the monitor, I saw a freeze-frame of Mom and him standing on a beach in Dana Point. They looked incredibly happy. Oh boy, he was at it again. Those stupid home movies.

"Dad, what are you doing?" I said.

"Wha?"

"Don't you have to go to work?"

Mom had once told me men needed constant supervision, or they tended to go off the reservation. She compared them to bowling balls and said women were the bumper rails. Seeing him like this proved she was right.

He stretched and yawned. "What time is it? Hey, I want to show you something."

Grabbing my hand, he sat me down at the computer and, leaning over my shoulder, moved to the beginning of the video he'd been assembling all night. As I watched in disbelief, a strange, disjointed flood of images appeared—a wedding, a honeymoon, family gatherings, and assorted vacations. They were chronological and mind-numbingly prosaic. The whole thing looked like a documentary on the narwhal. When it was over, I sat there, stunned and unable to speak.

"So, what do you think?" he said.

"Um..."

"When I show this to your mom, she'll see what a great family we had—*have*—and she won't marry—"

"Mom's getting *married*?"

I felt like someone wearing golf shoes had kicked me in the stomach. Dad got a panicked look on his face.

"Oh, boy," he said.

"Is it Warren? I'll bet it's Warren."

"Look, I'm sure I got it wrong. They're probably just friends." He tried taking my hands. "I'll make breakfast."

"When is all this supposed to happen?" I said, pulling away.

I felt feverish and suddenly had trouble swallowing. And what was that wart doing on my elbow? I never had a wart before!

"Never. Forget I said anything. Come on, let's eat."

"I mean, I knew she was moving on and all, but... And anyways, how can she marry that French-cuffed, mono-grammed, Brooks Brothers-wearing poser who thinks he can fly?"

"Rube, come on. It's a long time from now—in the future. I mean, you know your mother. This is a phase. She'll come around. You'll see."

He was beginning to sound delusional, like the time he tried convincing Mom and me that "It's a Small World" was the greatest ride ever invented.

"This can't be happening!"

Great, I was hysterical. I never get hysterical. Dad looked at me with the helplessness of an adult trying to remove a child safety cap. Then, he put on one of his famous smiles.

"Rube, once your mother sees this video, she'll—"

"She'll *what*, Dad? Do you honestly think this...experimental film is going to save our family?"

"Wait till I add the music."

"Oh!"

I felt disgusted. A seething rage I'd never known before consumed me. I headed straight for my room.

"It just needs some fine-tuning," he said.

It took me a while to calm down. After I had showered and dressed, I went to the kitchen to grab something before heading out to meet Claire and Diego. Dad was talking into his phone, which was lying on the counter on speaker, as he spooned an enormous dollop of Welch's grape jelly into a mixing bowl full of instant oatmeal. He hadn't even shaved yet.

"Gina? Alan."

He was doing his best to make his voice sound hoarse and painful. Actually, he was pretty convincing. Gina fell for it.

"Alan, I hardly recognized you," she said. "Are you sick?"

"I woke up with this throat thing. Probably caught it from Ruby. Can you tell Rick?"

"Yes, I'll tell him. Alan, I am so sorry. I hope you feel better. Are you taking Airborne?"

"I have to go, Gina. Bye."

"Grabbing a juice box," I said, heading for the refrigerator. "Thanks for blaming me for your fake illness, by the way."

He pointed at my backpack. "Going out? I made you breakfast."

He offered me the oatmeal. It looked grotesque in the way that fried mealworms look grotesque.

"Thanks. But Diego's mom is waiting downstairs. We'll be at the beach all day, okay?"

"Santa Monica?"

"Orange County somewhere."

"Claire going?"

"Of course."

"Make sure you stay with Diego's mom."

"I will." He was looking at me strangely. "What?"

"There's so much I don't know about you," he said. "You're fourteen and in high school, and you have your own life. There's Claire. And Diego. I have no idea where he fits in. Sorry, bad choice of words."

"I have to go."

"Sure. Don't let me keep you."

"Hey, Dad. We were going to try and find a dog beach, but since you're not going in today, can Ed stay with you? Thanks."

He tried the oatmeal, made a face, and added more grape jelly. I imagined my father thought the women in his life were abandoning him left and right. Okay, probably my guilt talking. I felt like I had to say something, though.

"I love you, Dad."

"Love you, too, Rube."

"Bye. Bye, Ed."

The dog followed me to the door. At least Dad would have some company. You know, misery and all that.

WE HAD an awesome time at Huntington Beach. It wasn't too crowded, and even though the waves were choppy, we had fun. After riding boogie boards, we rented bikes and cruised along the bike path singing "The Time Warp." Diego's mom treated us to Ruby's Diner on the pier, where I ate the biggest burger of my life. It was late afternoon, and we were parked at the curb in front of my dad's building. We'd already dropped Claire at her house.

"*Gracias,* Sra. Rivera," I said.

"*De nada, Reina,*" she said. She always called me that; I didn't know why.

I tried slipping her twenty bucks for gas, but she refused

it and gave me a kiss. As Diego and I exited the Honda Civic and headed for the front entrance, I tucked the twenty in his shirt pocket. He had insisted on carrying my backpack. So not cool, but very gentlemanly.

"I had fun, Diego. Thanks."

"Me, too. Hey, it's not so bad. Look at me. My mom and I are doing good."

I appreciated what he was doing. Earlier, I had told Claire and him the whole sordid tale about Mom possibly getting remarried. When the words came out, I wanted to cry. But I laughed instead and tried to make the whole thing sound absurd, in the French sense.

"Yeah," I said. "Guess I need to get used to living in Bizarro World." As I listened to my own voice, I felt like I could have been talking about amputating a limb.

"You'll be okay, Ruby. You're strong."

"That's me. 'Ruby the Rock.' See you, Diego."

"*Hasta luego.*"

He hesitated, as if waiting for something. I looked down at my shoes, then at him. This was becoming awkward. Finally, he shrugged and headed back to the car. Weird. Whatev'. I waved and, slinging my backpack over my shoulder, ran inside toward the elevator. As I got out my key to the apartment, the door flew open. Dad was standing there proudly, barefoot, unshaven, and wearing a chocolate-stained T-shirt and sweatpants. He looked gross. Even Ed was avoiding him.

"Prepare to be amazed!" he said.

This couldn't be good. Deliberately, I squeezed past him, set down the backpack, and went into the kitchen for a glass of milk. As I poured it, he hovered over me like a coffee-swilling Dementor.

"It's incredible what happens when you go back. You see

everything you did wrong."

"Dad, I'm really not in the mood. And, no offense, but you stink."

"Yeah, well. Who needs a shower when you're creating a masterpiece? Right, Ed? Come on, Rube, please? I made brownies!"

Groaning, I allowed myself to be dragged into the home office.

Chomping on a brownie, Dad paced as I tried getting comfortable in his office chair. I didn't want to be there and wondered how convincing I would be faking appendicitis. I tried the brownie, tasted butt, and spit it back onto the plate. Then, I gargled with milk and moved the mouse around.

"It's that button there," he said, reaching for the mouse.

"I know which button it is."

I started the video, and what followed was like a magic mushroom-fueled hallucination. It was Tim Burton meets the Lumière brothers. It was what happens when Oompa Loompas smoke all the Easter grass.

"Whoa," I said.

"Pretty compelling, huh?"

Dad was like a toddler who'd made his first potty, innocent and proud. Never mind that he did it in the fish tank. Though I didn't love the idea, I knew what I had to do. When you see a cancer, you have to cut it out or the patient will die. Dr. Ruby to the rescue! I cleared my throat, picked Ed up, and set him on my lap. I think the dog was starting to sense a pattern.

"Dad, listen," I said. "This is even worse than the last version. I can't tell you how bad it is. It's almost unreal. I mean, did you ever see *Norbit*?"

"Okay," he said.

"It's the worst thing ever. Right up there with *That's My*

Boy."

"I get it. Thanks for the feedback."

I got up and, avoiding eye contact, went to the door. Then, I stopped and faced my father, my stomach churning from the combination of the toxic brownie and the look of hopeless disappointment on his face. I was the worst kid ever.

"It's just that, I don't ever want to lie to you," I said. Only, in this case, it would have been better to lie like a rug.

"No, I know. It's fine. Really."

He tried hugging me, but I had to back away. I found myself using the "Mom finger."

"Okay, first, that project won't bring Mom back. And second, you really need a shower."

Later in my room, I Skyped with Claire and Diego. They were mostly sympathetic.

"You should have seen him. It was pathetic."

"Ruby, he loves your mom," Claire said. "What's wrong with you?"

I shook my head. "Seriously, I think he's losing it. Ever since he found out Mom is going to legit divorce him."

Diego tried consoling me. "I know it seems bad, but it will get better."

"Guys, I don't know what to do."

"Try having a little faith," Claire said.

Diego made a face. "It's not your job to fix this, Ruby."

"But I want to. I *need* to. I just don't know how."

That night I was so upset, I couldn't work on my machinima project. As I lay in bed, I stared at the ceiling. The stain had become a menacing creature in a hat. I thought I heard Mr. Shivers whispering. "Nuts to you, Wes," he said, like an assassin.

For the first time in my young life, I was truly scared.

7

"I'm not gonna hurt ya. I'm just gonna bash your brains in."

— THE SHINING

S everal long, hot days had passed. Dad and I had kept our distance, with me in my bedroom working on my machinima and Dad at the dealership all day. At night, he stayed in his home office editing his own personal, from-the-heart *Gigli*. Both Claire and Diego had advised me to give him time. I wasn't sure an eternity could fix this.

"You insulted his movie," Claire had said. "That was pretty harsh."

Diego had disagreed. "He's a guy. He'll get over it. Move on."

After walking the dog in the morning, I found Dad sitting in the breakfast nook, slurping coffee and reading the Sports section. Though he'd shaven, he looked like a dug-up corpse, wearing the suit he'd been buried in. I did my best to act nonchalant and started some raisin toast, but anyone with half a brain could have told you I was faking, because —unlike television actors who usually indicate nonchalance by whistling a non-existent tune—I hung my head and swung my arms like a caveman. Weird, right?

"Morning, baby," he said.

Wait, was he being pleasant?

"Hey, Dad."

Feeling like someone had rolled a huge boulder off me, I straightened his tie for him. He smiled and patted my head.

"Didn't you get any sleep?" I said. He gave a vague grunt. "Dad, I've been thinking. And I have a solution."

I noticed he was back to ignoring me and pinched his arm. "Dad!"

"Ow! What?"

"You need to call Matt."

"My brother? Why?"

"He can help you."

He put down the paper, rinsed his cup in the sink, and mimed looking for his car keys, even though they were lying right in front of him on the counter. No matter, I was fired up.

"Dad, stop pretending you don't know what I'm saying. It's very annoying. You need to call Matt now. He's a film-maker. He can totally get your project back on track."

"I'd rather swallow razor blades."

I knew he and Matt were not on the best of terms, but I soldiered on. "Come on, what better person to fix your movie?"

Oops.

"Hey, I can fix my own movie, thank you very much. I have to go to work."

He bent down awkwardly, pecked me on the forehead, and walked out, pointing at my elbow.

"You might want to have that wart looked at."

"It's not a wart!" I said, covering my elbow self-consciously. "Anyways, you'll think about it?"

When the door slammed, I turned back to my toast and noticed a shiny butcher knife lying on the counter.

"That reminds me..."

STACEY SAT AT HER COMPUTER, updating a formula in an Excel pivot table, though her mind was elsewhere. Since launching the new campaign, Viper Leather Goods' sales had shot up in a number of major markets, in spite of the soft economy. That should have made her happy, yet she felt empty and stared out the window at nothing. Her head hurt. She examined her left hand and noticed a faint depression where her wedding band had once been.

"I have a cure for that," someone said.

She looked up and saw Warren smiling at her. Lately, he had been putting on the pressure, and she was beginning to feel claustrophobic.

"I can't tell you how much I want to see my ring on your finger," he said.

"Oh, Warren. I'm still trying to figure it out. Besides, I can't wear it yet."

"You could wear it on another finger," he said, taking a seat on the corner of her desk and wiping a spot off his Bruno Magli tassel loafer with his thumb. "You've been alone too long, Stacey. It's time to act. Oh, and I need that forecast by COB today."

He left as quickly as he had come in. It always amazed her how easily he could glide between personal and business, as if he saw no distinction. Perhaps for him there was none.

She got out the diamond ring, as she had dozens of times over the last few days, and tried to see her future in the brilliant facets.

RICK VAN LOON surveyed the lush landscape of his showroom floor. In addition to his injured eye and fingers, he was now wearing a cervical collar. He noticed an unusual number of beautiful women looking at cars. *So many to choose from*, he thought with pointed frustration. *Why couldn't I have been born with eight arms?*

Alan trudged in and continued past Gina.

"Hey, good morning," she said. "You look...great."

"Yeah, I feel great." He indicated Rick with a tilt of his head. "Another date?"

"Kickboxer." She smiled bitterly and snatched the handset from her buzzing desk phone. "Lexus of Santa Monica. How may I direct your call?"

Alan recognized the jazz vocalist from Catalina's across the room, checking out a convertible. She was wearing a pink suit and carrying a matching Michael Kors bag. She met his eyes and smiled. His first instinct was to run. The last thing he needed was some romantic entanglement. Scanning the showroom, he saw that the other salespeople were engaged. Manning up, he straightened his tie and walked deliberately toward her, his hand extended warmly.

"Hi, I'm Alan Navarro."

"Laraine Moody."

He noticed she had large hands, and there was something unusual about her speaking voice.

"This is a very nice vehicle," he said. "Would you like to get in?"

"Sure."

He opened the door for her and waited as she made herself comfortable behind the steering wheel. Then, he plopped in next to her as she fiddled with the stereo. When he saw her Adam's apple, he realized she was trans.

"You don't want this sound system," he said. "I know a guy. He'll build you the sweetest little after-market setup."

"Do you remember me?"

"Catalina's, right? I love your voice. Thanks for the beer, by the way."

Resting a hand on his knee, she turned the dial to the jazz station 88.1. Ella Fitzgerald's "They Can't Take That Away From Me" poured from the speakers.

"Please don't," he said.

The words got under his skin and clawed at his veins. They reached around his heart and ripped it out whole, still beating. Alan was weeping uncontrollably now, mouthing the words to the song. Laraine snapped the radio off, her mouth falling open.

"Hey, what's wrong?"

"They say they can't, but they can!" he said, wiping his eyes with the heels of his hands. "They *can* take it away!"

"I know what you mean."

"I never wanted her to go. I thought we were happy."

"You give and give."

"She wanted to stay at home with a baby. But everyone has to work, right?"

"Why should you bear the whole burden?"

"It's not fair!"

By this time, a crowd of salespeople and customers had gathered. Gina watched from her desk, dumbstruck, as Alan poured his heart out to a customer. The next thing Alan knew, Rick was standing outside the passenger door, his hands on his waist. Alan looked up at him miserably. He and Laraine exited the vehicle, and Alan allowed himself to be led away by Rick and Gina.

"I hope everything works out," Laraine said.

Another salesman took charge and deftly directed her toward a pricey SUV she wasn't interested in.

Rick poured a cup of coffee from his ultra-expensive machine that heated the water to one hundred eighty degrees, the same as Starbucks extra-hot. He felt exhilarated, and wished he could chicken-walk across the showroom floor. Alan Navarro—the man who could make him feel like a schmuck with a single, off-handed remark—had messed up big. He smiled with phony sympathy that dripped like 30W motor oil as he handed the cup to his star salesman, who was now sitting in Rick's office, a broken man.

"What the hell happened out there?" he said. "Never mind, I don't wanna know. Take some time off, get therapy, whatever. Forget about the sales contest. There'll be other contests."

"Lots of contests," Alan said, unable to feel his legs.

As he wobbled to his feet and dragged himself to the door, he watched Gina and the other sales people pretending to be busy. *They'll be talking about this for weeks.*

Rick was practically salivating as he stood to deliver the coup de grâce.

"Alan, before you go," he said, "I've been meaning to ask. Do you think you might give me Stacey's cell number? I'd like to call her up for a cup of coffee. You know, just a casual thing."

His cheeks burning, Alan confronted the evil that was

Rick. For a second, he thought he had heard wrong. Yet there Rick was, standing in front of him and smiling, holding a pen and a notepad.

"*I'll* get you some coffee, Rick."

Alan marched stiffly to the credenza and, grabbing the steaming pot of fresh-brewed java, poured it down Rick's pants as his boss screamed in ear-splitting agony.

"Aieeeeee! You crazy— You're fired! Do you hear me? *Fired!* Oh, and I'll press charges, buddy! You bet I will! *Gina!*"

Gina dropped her poppy seed bagel and ran into Rick's office. Everyone in the showroom—including Laraine—watched as Alan stormed out. Seeing him this way made the bruises on her own body hurt again, and she realized today wasn't a good day to buy a car.

A Sammy Day messenger, who was ripped and wore tight red shorts, knocked on Alan's door, which set off a yapping dog alarm. Sammy Day Courier Service's motto was "What're you worried? You'll get it." When he didn't get an answer, he tried his special knock. Still nothing. As he grabbed a white plastic envelope and leaned it against the door, a tall man holding a Shih Tzu answered, looking about as presentable as Evil Ash in *Army of Darkness*.

"Mr. Navarro?" the messenger said, a little afraid.

"Hey."

Alan hadn't been expecting a package. Freeing up a hand, he took it. It was from the law offices of O'Brien, O'Brien & Wang. He didn't like the look of it. After signing, he was about to close the door when he thought of something.

"Hey," he said. "Got a few minutes?"

"Um, I have other deliveries."

"No-no-no, this isn't anything... I want to show you something I'm working on. I could use an outside opinion."

"I dunno, man...,"

"It's a movie."

The messenger's eyes brightened. "A movie? Interesting."

"I made brownies."

"Ooh, I love brownies!"

Sitting at Alan's computer, the Sammy Day driver, whose nametag read CARL, picked at a hangnail as Alan's hot mess of a home movie finished. He pounded down another brownie and drained his glass of milk. Then, he rubbed at the imaginary pain at the back of his neck. Being a successful salesman, Alan was very good at body language and sensed what was coming. Ed was sitting at attention next to the driver, and he gave the dog a quick pat.

"I would never pay to see this," Carl said, picking the last chocolate crumbs off his plate with a wet pinky.

"Why not?"

"Boy, where do I start? There's no arc. Where's your three-act structure? And who am I supposed to be following?"

Alan was getting steamed. Clearly, this rube was missing the point.

"Are you an idiot? There's no arc. These are my home movies!"

Never one to take crap off his three older brothers or anybody else, Carl pinned Alan against the wall with a furry forearm. The dog ran around in circles, barking.

"Who are you calling an idiot?" he said. "I've got a year of film school."

"Sorry," Alan said. "I'm a little tense. How about another brownie?"

Carl released him. "You got any real movies?"

RUBY HERE. I'd been hanging out with Claire and Diego at the Sherman Oaks Galleria. I know, I know! Old and cheesy, right? Well, I still liked it. When I walked into the apartment with my bags, I found Dad and some messenger dude sitting on the living room sofa with Ed on his lap, immersed in *Casablanca*. And of course, it had to be the scene where Rick puts Ilsa on the plane. I never cared much for romantic movies, but Dad loved them and used to always make me watch them with him when I was little. I can't tell you how many times I've sat through *The End of the Affair*.

Anyways, I didn't know what was happening, but these two doofs were crying like little girls and hadn't seen me come in. Dad offered his new movie buddy a tissue. By the time Rick said, "Here's looking at you, kid," they were holding each other and bawling like babies. Well, I couldn't take it anymore and broke up the party.

"What's going on?" I said.

Both of them turned crimson and got to their feet in a hurry. Dad fumbled for the remote and switched to ESPN while the other dude looked for the exit.

"I gotta go," he said, handing me his used tissue.

Clumsily grabbing his bag, he gave me the guy nod and headed out the door. When I looked at my father, my mouth hanging open like it had come off its hinges, he smiled awkwardly.

"I'm, uh, I'm just going to call Matt," he said.

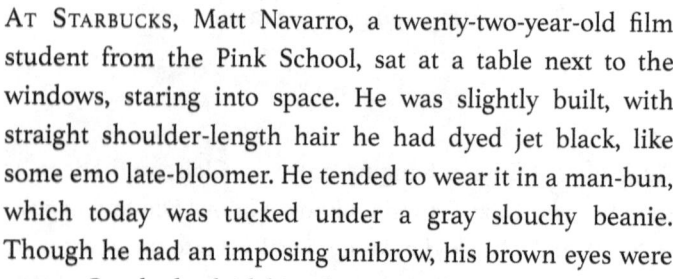

At Starbucks, Matt Navarro, a twenty-two-year-old film student from the Pink School, sat at a table next to the windows, staring into space. He was slightly built, with straight shoulder-length hair he had dyed jet black, like some emo late-bloomer. He tended to wear it in a man-bun, which today was tucked under a gray slouchy beanie. Though he had an imposing unibrow, his brown eyes were warm. Gently, he laid his phone on the table and sighed deeply, marveling at how one phone call could change your life.

Carrying two macchiatos, Phoebe Conklin came over and, sitting next to him, got her laptop out of her backpack. She was twenty-one, smart and pretty, with natural black hair, blue eyes, and creamy, pale skin. She was taller than Matt and, from the looks of her, definitely could have done better.

"Matt, here's the latest budget," she said, facing her laptop toward him. "I don't think I can cut any more—"

"This movie's gonna happen, Phoebe," he said, ignoring the screen.

"Well, yeah, eventually. We'll find the additional funds."

"No. I mean it's happening *now*."

He stared at her with a kind of crazed excitement that made her uncomfortable. Then, his eyes got huge, and he took her hand.

"I'm so friggin' happy!" he said.

8

"I think I must have one of those faces you just can't help believing."

— PSYCHO (1960)

"I'm sorry, man, but your movie is lame," Matt said after noisily slurping up the last of his broad noodles and wiping his chin with the back of his hand.

We were sitting around the dining room table. Dad had invited his brother and girlfriend/producer Phoebe over for Thai. Though he was technically my uncle, he had once cautioned me never to call him "Uncle Matt." Said it made him feel ancient.

So far, we had managed to avoid the topic of the infernal, dreaded home movie, which I had been forced to sit through again, and talked instead about the car business, sports, and film school. But when we did get around to the movie, Matt was merciless. Not even a shit sandwich for his big bro. You know what I'm talking about, right? *I see what you were trying to do. It's total crap. Good effort, though.* Mm, tasty.

Though originally this had been my idea, I was beginning to regret my decision. Dad hated Matt. Maybe it was because they came from different mothers. Also, I wasn't too sure how *I* felt about him. He struck me as a vain, immature rich kid who was so full of himself, it was coming out his ears. I mean, seriously. Who wears a Heisenberg to dinner? I hate hats, by the way. And he must have used *derivative*, like, ten times. Somebody get me a frying pan! But Ed loved him and spent the whole dinner curled up at my uncle's feet.

"I think it's sweet," Phoebe said.

I liked her. She seemed caring and sensitive to other people's feelings.

"Maybe with some better editing."

Dad smiled and finished his beer. "No, Matt's right," he said. "It was an idea. I'll think of something else. Vogon poetry or…"

For a split second, I thought that might actually work, seeing as Mom was such a huge fan of *The Hitchhiker's Guide to the Galaxy*. Putting that thought aside, I gathered up the dishes and rinsed them off in the sink.

"Dad, it's not that we don't love the concept." I was determined to make that sandwich.

"Yeah," Matt said. "I think there might be one or two good ideas."

He didn't sound very enthusiastic, and I was getting pissed. *What an arrogant little…* I needed to calm down, for Dad's sake. As I cleared the rest of the table, Phoebe placed the rinsed dishes in the dishwasher, gathered up the trash, and poured it into a garbage bag. I could tell that between Matt and her, she was the adult.

"I like your earrings," she said. "Where'd you get them?"

"Brandy Melville. They weren't expensive."

"Well, I love them."

"Here," I said. "Try them on."

"No... Really?"

"Sure."

As I handed them to her, I noticed Matt at the table, thrumming his fingers and obviously bored to tears. Why had Phoebe decided to hook up with this major loser? I mean, he was family and all, but she was better than that.

"Why don't you make a real movie?" Matt said to Dad out of the blue.

Dad was playing spin the bottle with his empty beer. "Real movie?"

"Yeah, a *real movie*. Something with a dramatic punch that will knock Stacey on her butt."

I knew instinctively the guy was a jerk, but this was something I hadn't expected. Despite my effort to stay calm, my heart beat faster. Then, I felt a rush. It was like riding Guardians of the Galaxy for the first time.

Before I could stop myself, I said, "That would be awesome!"

"Whoa, whoa," Dad said, looking at me like I had grown a second head. "You mean like an actual *movie* movie? Matt, you can't be serious. Wouldn't that cost a boatload of money?"

Phoebe hurried back to the table and sat. "Well, Matt and I have access to a lot of resources through the film school." She pointed to the earrings.

"Yeah, and Phoebe's great," he said, ignoring the jewelry. "She's already produced, like, eight student films."

From the look on Phoebe's face, I could tell she wasn't used to getting compliments from this guy, and seemed to be a little embarrassed. Smelling blood in the water, Matt continued.

"We wouldn't shoot on film, of course. We'd use hi-def video. That way, we can edit everything on a Mac using Final Cut Pro. It's pretty economical and will save us a ton of time."

Having hung around the dealership a lot, I knew a presumptive close when I heard one. He had said "*will* save us a ton of time." It didn't matter; I was all in.

"Dad, you have got to do this."

Matt must've attended a pitch workshop recently because he was like a machine. My mouth hanging open, I watched as he leaned in close and lowered his voice.

"The timing on this is pretty good," he said.

I thought he was going to finish the thought. Instead, he leaned back, relaxed, and smiled at Phoebe.

"Look, Alan, I'll be honest. I need to do a final project for school, and I've been having trouble coming up with a good story. I was hoping we could help each other?"

After what seemed like an eternal silence, Dad got out of his chair, went to the refrigerator, and brought over fresh beers for Matt, Phoebe, and himself. Then, he walked around the table. He had to be thinking the same thing I was. How had we gone from boring home movie to big-time Hollywood production?

"I don't know," he said. "What about equipment?"

Phoebe smiled. "Not a problem."

"Actors?"

"We have a regular troupe we work with."

"What about locations? Where can we even—?"

"Leave everything to me," Phoebe said, folding her arms.

Matt belched, which was unprofessional at best. At the workshop, he must've slept through the session on etiquette.

"Alan, think of this as your own personal, from-the-heart date movie."

"Can you imagine?" Dad said. "The dwarf sitting in the middle of a packed movie theatre in Westwood, about to spontaneously combust as people stand and applaud through the end credits!"

"Who's the dwarf?" Phoebe said.

I leaned over. "This loser my mom is supposed to be marrying." I shuddered for effect.

"Ahh..."

"No, forget it," Dad said, suddenly very serious. "How is a movie supposed to save my marriage? This is crazy. I can't believe we wasted so much time talking about it."

He plopped into his chair and picked at the label of his beer bottle. For a time, we sat there, sullen. I turned to Matt, who was smiling weirdly. Something told me the pitch wasn't over.

"No crazier than you trying to save your marriage with a home movie," he said. "But whatever."

"I'm telling you, Matt, it's nuts! N-v-t-s, nuts!"

"*History of the World: Part I*," Matt said, laughing at the reference. "Come on, Phoebe. We'd better get going." Then to Dad, "Thanks for the meal."

"Yes, thank you so much," Phoebe said, looking disappointed.

Dad rubbed his eyes. "Guess I'll figure something out. Thanks for making that long drive."

I felt awful and wanted to get back to my machinima project. It was the only thing that made sense to me now. When I looked at Matt, though, I noticed he was studying Dad in the same way a sociopath picks out his next victim.

"Alan, let me ask you something," he said. "When you go to sell a new car, do you use cheesy hand-drawn cartoons on toilet paper or professionally produced brochure-ware? I'm just sayin'."

"You already know the answer. And you went too far with the 'toilet paper' reference." Dad checked his watch. "Look, it's late. I'm sure everybody's tired."

"Yeah," Matt said, showing his disappointment. "We should go."

I watched as Phoebe and Matt gathered up their things. Dad was sulking at the table. I elbowed him and tilted my head toward our guests.

"What?" he said.

"Ask them if they want to crash here." Honestly, men were hopeless. Bumper rails, people!

"Oh, yeah."

He got up from the table and, as Ed and I followed, stopped Matt and Phoebe at the door.

"Hey, you guys are welcome to stay the night. No use you driving all that way."

"Are you sure it's not inconvenient?" Phoebe said.

"I would love it if you stayed. You can take the sofa and Matt can use a sleeping bag."

"Thanks, bro," Matt said. "Maybe I can come up with some ideas for your home movie."

I'll say one thing for Dad's brother: when he stuck you with the shiv, he made sure it stayed in.

I followed Dad into his home office and retrieved the sleeping bag from the closet, where I found a torn moving box with ALAN'S WRITING scribbled on the side in black Sharpie. Since when had Dad ever written anything? As I closed the closet door, Dad grabbed the priority envelope the messenger had left, ripped it open, and removed a thick packet of documents.

"What's that?" I said.

"Legal papers from Rick Van Loon's attorney. He's suing me." He flung the papers across the room. "Putz!"

I became worried. Would Mom and I lose the house?

"What are you going to do?"

"Nothing," he said. Then more to himself, "My own personal date movie."

He sat at his desk and returned to his hopeless video project. For a second, I watched as he played back one of the sequences Matt had pointed out as being "symptomatic of a larger problem." *Pretentious little...* Was this the sort of drivel they taught in film school these days? Shrugging, I grabbed the sleeping bag and returned to the living room. Phoebe was already snoozing on the sofa. Matt was sitting on the floor, reading something on his phone.

"Here," I said, handing him the sleeping bag.

"Thanks."

"Were you being serious when you said Dad could help with your movie?"

His eyes shifted toward Phoebe. "Um, sure."

"Huh."

"That thing he's working on is never gonna get your mom back. You know that, right?"

This guy had zero people skills. The flat tone in his voice was like ice water down my spine, and it made we want to hit him in the face with a croquet mallet.

"Thanks, Matt," I said, and headed quickly to my room, where I found Ed trying to climb up on the bed.

IT WAS early morning when that stupid bird woke me again. I was beginning to think Mom had sent it over from PetSmart. Instead of fighting it, though, I rose and got dressed. Mr. Shivers was nowhere in sight. And neither was the dog. Strange. In the living room, Phoebe was snoring softly on the sofa. Matt was lying on his back on the floor in the sleeping bag, his hat partially covering his face and drool leaking from his cake hole. Ed was curled up at his feet, and Mr. Shivers was perched on the arm of the sofa, leering. Silently, I grabbed the doll before Matt could wake up and die of a heart attack.

I hadn't even heard anyone come in. Suddenly, a manuscript with black covers, bound together by brass brads, landed on Matt's chest, startling him. The next thing I knew, Dad was looming over his brother like Grady in *The Shining*.

"I must be out of my mind," he said, half-smiling.

"What's this?"

Matt picked up the manuscript, and I caught a glimpse of the title: *Endless Honeymoon*.

"A screenplay? But how did you write—"

"College. I took a screenwriting class my junior year. It's a romantic comedy."

Matt turned to Phoebe, who was fully awake now and sitting up. For some reason, she looked uncomfortable as he thumbed through the script.

"It's perfect," he said.

I didn't know why, but I expected to hear an evil laugh.

WE HAD FINISHED a breakfast of pancakes and bacon. I had brought out my laptop and was showing Phoebe my machinima project. She seemed genuinely enthusiastic.

"This is so cool," she said. "I love machinima. I wish I

had the time, but... And you did all this yourself? What software are you using?"

"Machinima Studio and Blender. I'm playing around mostly. Trying to get the look right."

"Well, it's awesome. When you're finished, I can totally help you out with post. We can add some cool titles and library music."

"That would be amazing. Thank you!" I said.

Dad poured more coffee for Matt, Phoebe, and himself. I'd already finished my cup. Matt had the screenplay open as he took a swallow.

"Here's what's gonna happen," he said. "Phoebe and I will be gone for a bit. We have a lot of prep work. We'll be on the road mostly, but you've got our cell numbers."

"What can I do?" Dad said.

"Polish the script. You know, update it. Most of these references are pretty ancient."

"It could be a period film."

"No, forget it."

"We wouldn't be able to afford the cars and the clothes," Phoebe said.

Dad nodded. "Got it."

I continued working on my machinima in the kitchen. Phoebe and Matt were pacing in opposite directions in the living room. Dad watched them, a little in awe, as they engaged in separate animated phone conversations.

"Do you think this is how they spend their days?" he said to me.

"Huh?"

"What do they do for money? Wait. *Dad.* My father must be footing the bill for Matt's school. Who knows what other funds he's provided." Dad lowered his voice. "Listen, you can't tell your mother about any of this."

"Roger that. Speaking of which, what will you do about the money Matt needs? I mean, Rick did fire you."

"Guess I'm going to have to sell my jazz collection." When Dad saw the look on my face, he smiled. "Fortunately, I made some good investments. I can get by for a while. We'll finish the movie, get your mom back, and then, I'll figure something out."

"Sounds great, Dad," I said, cringing.

Outside in front of the apartment building, Phoebe and I talked favorite horror movies while I kept Ed on a leash. We were waiting for Matt to start his car, a vintage Mercedes. Dad leaned into the driver's side window. I could hear them talking.

"I'm impressed," Dad said. "I thought you'd have to pry the old man's cold dead fingers from the wheel."

Something must've changed. I remembered Dad telling Mom and me one time about how "frugal" his father was. Though Dad had always had everything he needed growing up, he couldn't recall a single time when his father had done something "just for the hell of it." There was always a quid pro quo.

"He handed me the keys when I totaled the MINI Cooper," Matt said.

"Wow, he never would have done that when he was with Mom."

"How come you never go see him?" Matt said.

"And his trophy wife?" He sounded a little bitter.

To hear Dad tell it, the breakup had happened when he was almost an adult, and had hurt him deeply. What was bad was seeing his mom carry on, pretending to be cheerful when she was with her friends and the priest Dad had known since he was a kid.

"Hey, my mom's been great," Matt said. He sounded defensive.

"Look, I didn't mean anything. Dad's moved on. From my mother, from me. There's nothing to talk about."

"No, I understand," Matt said.

"Yeah, water under the bridge."

As much of a jerk as my uncle was, I think he liked my dad. Dad had told Mom and me that Matt was an only child and might have craved a big brother. He was a small kid. One time in fifth grade he'd gotten a bad beating. No big brother to come to the rescue.

"He talks about you," Matt said. "I think he's proud of you."

"I'll send him a Christmas card."

"Right."

Dad straightened up and stretched. "Hey, Matt. I'm happy to put money into this thing, but I'm trusting you and Phoebe to keep the budget under control."

"You got it. Later, big bro."

Matt hit the horn. Phoebe hugged me and jumped into the car. Then to me, "Oh, your earrings!"

"Keep them," I said.

"Really?"

"Sure. For good luck."

"Thanks!"

Matt pulled away slowly as Dad and I did the corny wave thing like a couple of rubes.

"This better work," Dad said, smiling through clenched teeth.

"He's your brother, Dad. What could possibly go wrong?"

9

"I shot him six times! This guy, this man—he's not human!"

— HALLOWEEN II (1981)

The Geiger Asylum for the Criminally Insane was situated deep in the woods of the Pacific Northwest, far away from people and distant from practically anything living. Outside, no sounds of birds, raccoons, or chipmunks ever split the heavy silence, which hung like a low, poisonous fog. In a clearing, sprawling grounds surrounded a massive steel and concrete ten-story structure that had been erected in the 1950s, when it was popular to lobotomize patients who were violent. Someone once said when you enter this place you'd better pray you die quickly from a disease.

Inside, the constant wailing voices mixed with a sickly dripping noise kept the staff on edge. The huge desk in the guard station stood cluttered with stained coffee cups and empty takeout containers from the cafeteria. A half-moon of television monitors glowed with images of sorry inmates in small, dank cells, some talking to people who weren't there, others writing imaginary words in the air, and still others sleeping like corpses from all the medication.

A young rookie who had come out of a two-year training program at a local community college handed a coffee that smelled of burning rubber to a grizzled guard six months from retirement. How the old guard had managed to survive in this crypt was a mystery to the kid, who hoped this time his application to the police academy wouldn't be rejected.

"Thanks," the old guard said, taking a slurp. "You seen Frank?"

"He's prob'ly in the can again."

"Gotta be the coffee." Making a face, the old guard took another swallow.

The kid tilted his head at the video monitors. "You been by his cage?"

"Chuck? I try never to go down there anymore. Been watchin' him on the monitor, though. Look."

One of the screens—Number 11—displayed a dark, claustrophobic cell with a lifeless lump lying under a blanket in the middle of the bed. Unlike the other screens, Number 11 never took its electronic eye off the cell. In fact, it had been displaying the same gloomy scene for close to twenty years. The first time the old guard had seen it, after transferring from San Quentin, he noticed that Chuck rarely moved. He was always in some kind of trance. Perhaps it was better that way. Chuck was the most dangerous inmate they had. It was said he could control your mind and had the strength of ten men. The less anyone dealt with him, the better.

"I remember one time he grabbed this other inmate and

whispered somethin' to 'im. Later, that poor sorry SOB slammed his own head into a wall till it turned to Jell-O."

The old guard leaned in and, taking a closer look at the monitor, noticed something peculiar. Part of a black boot was sticking out from under the blanket. None of the inmates were allowed to wear shoes. Each had been issued a pair of soft slippers. For no reason, he thought of a glitch that had occurred a few minutes earlier. The screen had gone dark for several seconds. When it came back on, everything appeared normal, as if nothing had happened.

"Somethin's wrong," the old guard said, his pulse quickening. "Stay here!"

"Hey, I can go."

The old guard grabbed the kid's forearm and glowered. "Kid, you have no idea what you're dealin' with. That down there? He's the devil."

"You go, then."

A heavy iron door slammed open, and the old guard, armed with a riot stick and a powerful Taser, strode down a narrow corridor, keys jingling, as another guard carefully locked the door behind him. The wailing was deafening, echoing off the slick, moist walls. Desperate, deformed hands with black, razor-like fingernails protruded from the bars of the other cells, clawing at him as he passed.

Back in the guard station the kid, gnawing on a day-old cruller, watched in silent fascination as the old guard moved across the video monitors. Eventually, he appeared on Number II's screen. The camera facing Chuck's cell was mounted outside on the opposite wall, and the kid could see his partner approaching the cell door, his Taser gripped tightly in one hand. Inside, nothing moved.

The old guard took hold of a single key and unlocked the door. He entered the cell and locked the door behind him, something the kid would have been very reluctant to do. Slowly, he approached the bed and used his riot stick to push back the blanket. Over the radio, the kid heard his partner gasp and squinted into the monitor to try to see what the old guard was seeing.

His face ashen, the old guard turned around and stared directly into the video camera.

"It's Frank," he said, his voice tinny and unreal.

The kid blinked hard. "What the..."

He backed away from the monitor, unable to comprehend how a patient could have murdered a security guard and escaped his cell without being seen by anyone. Sensing a presence, he wheeled around. His face contorted into an image from a funhouse mirror, and he screamed. A fleshy tearing noise filled the guard station. Then, nothing.

The kid's pale hand, bloody and lifeless, fell onto a big red button with a sign above it that read IN CASE OF HELL, PRESS HERE.

Outside, it was pitch black and pouring rain. Sirens shrieked across the compound as bright searchlights scanned the darkness. Guards with high-powered rifles scattered like bugs as the old guard's angry voice shouted commands over a PA system that tended to break up a lot.

Somewhere on a remote forest road far from the asylum, the sound of labored breathing added a choppy undercurrent to the silence. A silhouetted figure in asylum-issue pajamas and slippers ran frantically through the rain toward the nearest town.

GRABBING MY CHEST, I shot straight up in bed. Outside my room, I could hear the wind blowing and tree branches hitting the window. My heart was beating like a humming-bird, and when the bedroom door opened, I let out a yelp. Whew, it was Dad!

"You okay, honey? I thought you called out."

I was fanning myself like an imperial concubine, trying to get my pulse down. "It was a stupid dream."

He bent down, picked up Mr. Shivers off the floor, and placed him back on the chair.

"Nuts to you, Wes!" the doll said.

"Dad!"

"Wow, I didn't even pull the string. Call me if you need anything."

"I'm fine now."

"Want a brownie?"

"No-uh!"

"Night."

As he closed the door, I lowered myself down and pulled the covers tight around my neck. This was ridiculous. I never got scared, even after watching *Ringu* with all the lights off when I was seven. There was no way I was getting any sleep, so I decided to do some work. Groaning, I dragged myself out of bed and opened my laptop cover. As the screen got brighter, I stared at the disturbing image of a machinima man in dirty pajamas running in the rain in an endless loop. But that wasn't the worst part.

I was pretty sure I'd never ever created that scene.

10

"Meat's meat, and man's gotta eat!"

— MOTEL HELL

The sky and the sea melted into an endless blue as Matt wound his way lazily up Highway 1. Though only twenty-two, he drove as if he were seventy, afraid of getting even a scratch on his father's prized Mercedes. And the fact that he was wearing a pale blue bucket hat did nothing to change the impression. He bit off another hunk of beef jerky and chewed loudly. Next to him, Phoebe read from her laptop, doing her best to ignore the irritating champing noise that reminded her of a dog gnawing gristle—lots and lots of gristle.

They had been together since their second year of film school. Phoebe was the organized one, while Matt was "the artist," creating a surprising number of short films—mostly horror—that were thin and, yes, *derivative*. During their first year, she had produced one of his shorts. But he had been insufferable. Nevertheless, she stayed on until they completed the movie because she was a professional. Later when asked about the experience, she had said he was an unkind, self-absorbed Guillermo del Toro wannabe, and vowed never to work with him again. Ever.

Then in their second year, he made *Last Dance*.

Matt wrote, shot, edited, and scored the movie. It was a love letter to a young girl with a weak heart named Marieke. A beautiful, happy child, she attended a traveling carnival with her friends and happened into a fortune teller's tent, where the strange woman warned her never to fall in love and be kissed—or she would die.

Three years later, a boy named Tru came into Marieke's life and, the warning long forgotten, she let him stay. He was beautiful and innocent and only wanted to make her happy. At their first high school dance under the soft lights, he kissed her. She died in his arms.

When Matt screened his film for the class, Phoebe wept. After that, she signed on to produce his next movie, and the next, and so on, hoping to experience the magic one more time. Unfortunately, he never showed that side of himself again.

Reading in the car always gave Phoebe motion sickness, but she carried on. The gum helped. Besides, staying focused on her laptop was a sure way to avoid catching the maestro picking his nose.

"It says here," she said, "that years ago Becker had a love affair with Nadia Ionescu during the filming of *The Sea, the Sand and the Sea*."

"She's next on my list," he said with a tone that once again suggested the oblique autocrat who thought he could pick up the phone and get any A-list actor in town.

"I'm not sure that's a good idea."

He ignored her as he signaled two hundred yards in advance of the next exit.

Denny's was filled with the usual number of customers, the main dining room populated by the slow, the disillusioned, and the road-tired. Phoebe continued reading from her laptop as Matt helped himself to more of her cherry pie. He was always stealing her food.

"Oh, boy," she said. "It goes on to say that after Nadia vanished, Becker went nuts. They arrested him in Central Park for reciting the Sears catalog naked and, get this, smearing his own feces on *Romeo and Juliet*."

"That ugly bronze sculpture? No way."

"It's not ugly, Matt."

She looked at him with the same concern she had had that time they broke into the Udder Delight brassiere factory at night to shoot the climax of their latest short, *Boobs in Toyland*.

"I don't think we can work with him," she said. "The guy's a total nutcase."

"Everything will be fine."

"Why does everyone keep saying that? Matt, seriously, what are we doing?"

"What do you mean?" he said, smacking his lips. "We're making a feature film. This is our dream, remember? Come on. We better get some gas."

As they rode on, he snapped his fingers impatiently. Without breaking her concentration, she dug through her purse and handed him a bent stick of Juicy Fruit gum.

"Aw, come on."

"It's that or the orange Tic Tac stuck to the bottom of my purse."

"I'll take the gum. So what was the last film Becker made?"

"Hang on..."

"Phoebe!"

She struggled with the pronunciation. *"Tod dem fetten wurstfressenden Arschloch!"*

"Die, You Fat Sausage-eating Bastard!" He snorted loudly, almost choking on his gum. "I love that friggin' movie. You do realize that was the last film Müller ever directed."

"Good thing," she said. "His entire oeuvre is garbage. Not to mention, the women in his movies are either babbling idiots with big breasts or crazy-eyed murderous grandmothers who like to quote *Mein Kampf.*"

"Has anyone ever told you, you have zero sense of humor?"

"You have. Frequently."

"Because it's true."

The German director Gert Müller had made a number of low budget films in the mid-seventies and early eighties, not one of which ever garnered a decent review. Each time a critic eviscerated one of his movies, he would hunt him down in a restaurant and beat him mercilessly until the police arrived. Eventually, everyone except foreign journalists using fake credentials and false beards refused to review his work.

The son of a successful pharmacist, Müller claimed the whole thing was political and that he was, in fact, a martyr for film and Marxism. In an interview with a British magazine, Wim Wenders had once provided a lukewarm defense of his countryman. When prodded by the insistent reporter, he said at last, "I think Gert means well." Eventually, Müller vanished from the scene and was never heard from again, much to the relief of filmgoers, critics, and weary tax collectors everywhere.

"I don't have a good feeling about this," Phoebe said,

examining an old headshot of the German actor Klaus Becker, who had starred in three of Müller's movies.

Phoebe hadn't told Matt the half of it. In addition to being Müller's favorite actor, Becker, too, was an unstable man with a serious drinking problem and prone to violent outbursts. He was born in Baden-Baden, and when he was thirteen, his parents immigrated to the United States. Decades ago, he had had a torrid love affair with Nadia Ionescu during the filming of *The Sea, the Sand and the Sea*, a minor epic about the Hungarian Revolution of 1956 that had been shot on the backlot at Warner Bros.

When Nadia disappeared mysteriously after the last day of shooting, Becker went insane. Months later, he was arrested in Central Park. One witness claimed the pigeons had given him a standing ovation. At his trial, Becker insisted on representing himself and tried mounting a freedom of speech defense. When that failed, he informed the judge confidentially that it was only doggy doo-doo. And besides, he had secured a permit.

After a court-ordered psychiatric evaluation, Becker received a suspended sentence and, during a chance encounter with a television producer at an AA meeting in Los Angeles, landed the role of Dr. Austin St. Claire on the long-running daytime drama *Roadside Hospital*, for which he received two Emmy nominations.

Though managing to remain sober, Becker was difficult to work with and frightened the cast and crew. A rumor that he was the real Zodiac Killer began making the rounds. Eventually, his contract ran out, and for several years after, he appeared in low-budget horror movies both here and abroad. While shooting *Tod dem fetten wurstfressenden Arschloch!*—his last film—in the Black Forest, he met Anna Zumwald at a café. He had gone to school with her as a child and learned her husband had died recently.

Soon after, Dario Argento offered Becker a role as a corpse in his next movie. Aware that his career was over, and not wanting to be compared to Kevin Costner in *The Big Chill*, the actor flew to Rome and pushed the scrawny Italian into a fountain on the Via Veneto, returned to Germany, married Anna, and brought her to the US. They took up residence north of Santa Barbara, where he ran his late parents' hog farm.

The next Christmas, Becker sent Argento a crate of frozen pork sausage with his compliments.

THOUGH IT WAS SUMMER, the surroundings were cool and darkly beautiful as Matt rolled to a stop in front of the faded main gate. Phoebe looked apprehensive as he stuck his head out and tried to make out the name on the rusty mailbox.

"Do you think she's still living with him?" she said.

"Aw, I can't read the friggin' name. What? Who?"

"*Anna*, his wife?"

"What am I, psychic? How should I know? This has got to be it. I'm going in."

He pulled the car up to the quaint farmhouse, scattering dirt and chickens. It was deathly quiet except for a chill wind in the trees that carried a faint squealing that reminded Phoebe of the demonic cries Matt had used in one of his early shorts, *Chicken Kiev*, which was about a timid man named Albert Kiev who had lost a bet and was forced to spend a terrifying night in a haunted poultry processing plant.

As Phoebe tried to guess the source of the noise, Matt

stepped on a rake and cursed as the wooden handle smacked him in the face. Suddenly, a gunshot sent a flock of blackbirds screeching into the harsh graying sky.

"Matt, seriously. I really don't have a good feeling about this."

Unnerved, he pretended he hadn't heard her and continued toward the house. As they approached the front door, she clung to his arm, making him wince. Both of them hesitated on the porch. As Matt rang the doorbell, Phoebe spotted a wooden rocking chair bleached by the elements. They waited. Nothing. Matt tried again. She thought she saw the chair move and swallowed hard. It had never occurred to her she would die in the middle of nowhere surrounded by dirt and chickens. She had always pictured Venice.

The light was fading, the sky becoming a rich indigo, as they made their way through the trees along a narrow dirt path. In the distance, Phoebe noticed a shed, and next to it, a pen containing around a dozen enormous hogs. The only sound she could hear was a rhythmic tearing noise coming from inside the shed.

"Hello?" Matt said. "Mr. Becker?"

The tearing noise ceased.

A tall man—Klaus Becker—stepped out, wearing black rubber boots, a black rubber apron, black gloves, and clear protective goggles. He looked to be around seventy, with a shock of steel gray hair. He was strange and dark-humored, with the haunting eyes of a Hessian ghost. He held a knife dripping with gore, and he was drenched in fresh pig's blood. Seeing the specter, Phoebe turned white and covered her mouth.

"I think I'm going to be sick."

She turned around and found Matt passed out on the

ground like a left-behind doll. When she looked up, she saw Becker moving toward her swiftly, still clutching the knife. Frozen, she screamed, but the sound was lost among the cruel trees.

"Let's get him back to the house," Becker said.

THE DINING ROOM was warm and inviting with good, heavy furniture. Only one photograph stood on an antique sideboard. It was of Becker and a kind-looking woman who might have been in her late fifties. At the table, Phoebe and Matt tore into their sausage and potatoes as Becker poured out more lemonade from a glass pitcher. Wanly, he flipped through the black-covered screenplay in front of him.

Phoebe cleared her throat. "Is Mrs. Becker here?"

Not looking up, the German answered her vaguely. "She died under mysterious circumstances."

"Oh?"

"This sausage is great," Matt said, a piece of potato falling onto his shirt.

The man is utterly clueless, Phoebe thought.

"I make it myself," Becker said. He closed the screenplay and regarded it without enthusiasm. "*Chainsaw Chuck*."

His voice sounded like a weary train conductor announcing the next station, which happened to be Lompoc.

Matt pointed at the screenplay with his knife. "We want you to play the caretaker."

Becker waved his hand dismissively. "A student film."

"A horror movie," Phoebe said, trying to brighten the mood.

Becker sighed heavily. "I prefer romantic comedies."

After dinner, Phoebe and Matt sipped coffee from red-and-white bone china mugs as Becker stoked the fire in the comfortable living room, which was filled with books. Though it was summer, the night felt cold. On the mantle stood another photograph of Mrs. Becker, taken much later. She was sitting alone in the old rocking chair on the porch, with a woolen shawl covering her frail shoulders, her eyes milky and distant. Phoebe startled when she realized she was resting against that same shawl, which was now draped over the back of her chair.

The German considered the hot poker. Then, he looked grimly at the two hopeful young filmmakers.

"I'm retired," he said, handing back the screenplay.

Phoebe stood to take it. "But you'd be—"

Matt grabbed her arm as if she were a child about to put her hand into an open flame. She had no idea what he was up to, but decided to stand down. She watched as he smiled resignedly at Becker.

"Nadia warned us you wouldn't do it," Matt said.

Becker looked at him sharply. "Nadia Ionescu? You spoke to her?"

"Yes, back in LA." Matt was an inveterate liar, a talent he took pride in. "She was sure you wouldn't want to see her again. But I refused to listen. I told her enough time had passed since—"

"That's right," Phoebe said, getting into the spirit. Unlike Matt, she was terrible at lying, especially under pressure. "Since *The Sand, the*—"

"*The Sea, the Sand and the Sea*?" Becker said, trying to be helpful. He prodded the fire a little more and replaced the poker. "You're both miserable liars."

"No, just her," Matt said, glaring at Phoebe.

Phoebe sighed. "Look, Mr. Becker. We want you in our

movie that's not a romantic comedy. Or anything remotely close."

"I did *Barefoot in the Park*!" Becker said, banging his fist on the mantle.

Matt helped himself to more coffee. "You crapped on a statue."

"Oh, no..." Phoebe covered her face and shook her head.

A leaden silence hung in the air like smog in the Forbidden City. Without warning, Becker burst into a frightening laugh that resonated throughout the house. The spasm took hold of him, and he had to use the mantle to support himself. He wiped the tears from his eyes with a crusty thumb.

Phoebe tried again. "We came here because we think you're perfect for this role."

Becker regarded her without expression. Uncomfortable, she turned away and looked at the photograph on the mantle. She could see herself in it now, wrapped in the shawl. Her hair was silver, and her eyes were distant and frightened. Her heart was beating like a dirt rammer, and she felt a small animal gnawing at her ankle.

"I'll do it on one condition," Becker said. "That you cast Nadia as my wife."

Matt stood. "Done!"

Her head swimming, Phoebe turned to him, confused. "Huh? We don't even—"

"I'll write down my phone number," Becker said. "You can call me when she accepts. Shall I bring my knives?"

As the German strode out of the room to find a pen, Phoebe stared at Matt, slack-jawed.

"Piece of cake," he said, full of himself as per usual.

11

"Vee had better confeerm de fect dat yunk Frankenshtein iss indeed vallowing een ees gandfadda's vootshtaps!"

— YOUNG FRANKENSTEIN

The school auditorium stage was a closed frightening forest. The hooting of invisible owls and the chittering of other unseen creatures seemed to come from everywhere. Intermittent lightning broke through the moody, cobalt blue firmament, followed by the ominous rumbling of distant thunder as Hansel and Gretel made their way timidly through the forest. The boy was dressed in a short woolen jacket and matching pants. The girl had on a shawl and skirt and wore a scarf on her head. Both were barefoot. They stopped when they heard a sudden tick-tick noise.

"Father, is that you?" Gretel said, her voice small and afraid.

Her brother took her hand. "Be quiet. It's only a bird."

As they followed the sound, the trees separated magically, revealing a small house made of bread and cakes. Weak with hunger, they tore off pieces of the house and ate them. As they worked their way to the front of the house, the door burst open, and a shabbily dressed, grotesque old woman appeared, supporting herself on wooden crutches.

"Who is nibbling at my house?" she said.

Frightened, the children screamed and ran offstage. Straightening up, the old woman lay down the crutches and pulled off her ugly mask, revealing another girl, a little older and very pretty.

Phoebe and Matt watched from the audience, rapt, as Nadia Ionescu approached the stage from the center aisle. She was in her late sixties, wore exaggerated vintage clothing from Melrose Avenue, and looked as if she might have a screw loose. She spoke in a dense Romanian accent that reminded Matt of the European horror movies he loved.

"All right, Ian. What happened?" Nadia said. "Ian and Faaizah?"

Meekly, the children playing Hansel and Gretel returned to the stage.

"She scared us," Faaizah said, digging her bare toe into the imaginary soil of the forest floor.

Ian folded his arms and looked off into the middle distance. "*I* wasn't scared."

"It's good you felt real fear," Nadia said. "That means the audience will, too. Come, we'll try it again, yes?"

Ian pointed an accusing finger at the older girl. "She needs to open the door softer."

"Fine," Nadia said, sighing, even though she knew in her heart the witch had performed her part exceptionally.

"I have to pee," Faaizah said, crossing her legs and twisting from side to side.

Nadia looked up to the heavens. "*Ura si la sara!*"

Later in her cramped office at the prestigious Paternoster Academy, Nadia sat at her desk and warmed her arthritic hands around a steaming mug of green tea. Even though it was hot outside, the air conditioning always gave her a chill. The shelves behind her were filled with books, plays, and old photographs of family, friends, and deceased actors. On the wall hung a framed *The Sea, the Sand and the Sea* movie poster. Phoebe and Matt sat across from her on a worn red velvet loveseat Nadia had discovered at a yard sale. He was wearing a light gray straw diamond porkpie hat. Impatient, he jumped in, dispensing with the normal pleasantries.

"So we were—"

"I love *Hansel and Gretel*," Phoebe said, cutting him off. "I didn't know the school had a summer program."

"Yes, we perform year round."

"How many plays have you staged?"

"Oh, too many," Nadia said, brushing away the memory with her hand. "The children do seem to enjoy it, though. We were written up in the *Los Angeles Times* last year."

"I remember! Um, as you know, we're from the Pink School."

"I don't do student films," Nadia said, smiling professionally. She turned to her copy of the play and made some notes in the margins.

"No, we— We wanted to ask you about Klaus Becker."

Nadia dropped her pen and looked sharply at Phoebe. "Why?"

"We're studying *The Sea, the Sand and the Sea*, and we read that you and he were kind of, um, together a lot. All the time, actually."

Nadia rose stiffly and poured more hot water into her cup. It annoyed Matt that she hadn't used a fresh tea bag.

"That was a long time ago," she said. "And I suppose you also want to know why I left? Everyone does."

Matt had had enough and took charge. "Here's the deal. Klaus Becker is playing the caretaker in our movie."

Nadia glared at him defiantly. "Why are you telling me?"

Phoebe shot him an angry look and did her best to recover, fully aware the damage had already been done.

"We thought if we explained the situation," she said, "you might consider—"

The boy playing Hansel appeared. When he saw Phoebe and Matt, he stopped and lingered at the door.

"What is it, Ian?" Nadia said.

The boy, his hands folded behind his back, refused to look her in the eye. "I don't wanna be in the play."

"We'll discuss it later." Her voice was at once firm and loving.

Instead of going away, the boy came in and positioned himself in front of Matt, staring at him glumly. Taking her cue, Phoebe got to her feet and pulled Matt up.

"You're busy," she said. "How about if we leave you the script, and if you change your mind, you can call us."

She gingerly laid the screenplay on the desk. Though Nadia refused to look at it, Phoebe went on.

"We were hoping you would be the caretaker's wife."

Satisfied she had turned the situation around, she rejoined Matt and took his arm, intent on getting him out of there before he could do any more harm.

"The thing is," Matt said, ignoring Phoebe's nails digging into the back of his hand, "we don't have a lot of time—"

"Meanie," Ian said and kicked Matt in the shin as hard as he could.

"Ow!"

"Ian!" Nadia said.

Panicked, Phoebe yanked Matt out the door, and they left.

Later in her office, Nadia sat on her loveseat, her arms around Ian, the screenplay lying on her lap. Faaizah sat on her other side, looking at the cover and tracing over the title with her finger. Nadia stared at the script in silence, resisting the temptation to open it.

"Are you doing the movie?" Ian said.

"Sure. *La Pastele cailor*."

"What's that 'upposed to mean?"

Faaizah rolled her eyes and leaned over. "It means *never*, dumbo."

THOUGH IT WAS BLISTERING hot in downtown LA, the tall trees surrounding the exterior of the Los Angeles Public Library made it bearable. Phoebe and Matt walked up to the main entrance as the *paletero* with one leg shorter than the other passed them on Flower Street, his bell tinkling. Hungry, Matt made a move toward the cart, but Phoebe yanked him away by the arm.

"I can't believe it. You are such a, a...*dick*," she said.

"Oh, we're talking again?" He took his arm back. "Look, either she'll do the movie or she won't. And for your information, my leg is killing me."

"Serves you right, Matt. Those memories are obviously very painful for her. You can't just walk in there and— Oh, forget it."

Sitting at one of the long tables inside, Phoebe combed through a stack of magazines while Matt sat next to her, searching YouTube on his laptop. She opened a vintage movie magazine and flipped through it until she found the article she was looking for.

"Isn't everything on the Internet?" he said.

"Keep your voice down! Now, listen. It's the only interview she ever gave. 'I was so much in love, I wanted to run home to tell my parents. It was raining that day. Getting off the train in Bucharest, I slipped and hit my head. I was in a coma for weeks. When I awoke, I couldn't remember who I was.'"

"Oh, brother. Talk about your B-movie plot devices."

"Shut up. 'One day, I was riding a bus past the local cinema. They were showing *The Sea, the Sand and the Sea*. When I saw the title on the marquee and the movie poster, all my memories came flooding back. It had been two years! After that, I was too ashamed to contact Klaus.'"

"Sounds bogus to me."

Phoebe pressed her hand to her mouth. "That is so sad."

"Yeah, tragic. Come on, I'm starving."

At the nearby garage, Matt unlocked his car as Phoebe stood on the opposite side and gave him another of her looks, which he ignored.

"So here's my idea, right?" he said. "We get the name of that spiritual advisor she goes to. We slip her some cash, and she tells Nadia the friggin' stars are aligned to do our movie. What do you think?"

Phoebe scoffed. "You're out of your mind."

"You got any better ideas? Hey, I'm all ears over here."

"Let me handle it," she said. He shook his head. "I mean it, Matt. Stay away from Nadia."

"Whatever. Are we meeting my brother, or what?"

"Ruby texted me. They're waiting for us at Raleigh Studios."

"Don't forget, we're making a romantic comedy. Say it with me. Rom-com."

"I am not an idiot, Matt."

They each climbed into the Mercedes and slammed their respective doors, the sound echoing through the structure like the shutting of some gigantic cosmic portal.

RUBY HERE. Did you know I've lived in LA my entire life and have never actually been on a sound stage? True story. I took the Warner Bros. tour once, but they don't let you go anywhere good. I thought the place would be, you know, glamorous. But it didn't look anything like in the movies. Bright lights shone from the ceiling, and an expensive-looking video camera pointed at a tiny set, where everything was green.

I was surprised at how small the crew was. A guy with a boom mic was standing on the set. Some other dude wearing headphones sat at a cart with what I assumed was an audio recorder. A girl stood behind the camera, holding a script in one hand and a Sharpie in the other. The director and assistant director were standing next to another cart, looking at a video monitor. All in all, pretty boring, if you ask me.

Everyone else waited around, watching, as some actor named Louie De Niro (no relation) stood in front of the green screen, dressed as a British knight and waving a sword that, thanks to a mix-up at the costume rental company, I guess, turned out to be Spanish. I recognized it as Inigo Montoya's sword from *The Princess Bride*. I thought about saying something when I realized it probably didn't matter, since this was only a dumb commercial for mouthwash.

Louie looked to me like he might be in his mid-thirties. Sort of good-looking, though not so great with the words when he wasn't holding a script in his hand. He was the guy we were here to see. Matt was hoping to cast him as "Sam" in our movie. Judging from the expression on Dad's face, he was having a hard time picturing it.

This was the part where Louie was supposed to slay the Bad Breath Dragon, which was in reality a beach ball taped to the end of a long metal pole, held up by a bored crew member standing on a green ladder and also dressed in green from head to toe. Later, they would use CG to create the actual dragon. They had been at this for over an hour, and I don't think Louie was "feeling it."

"Mighty Dragon," he said, trying out an English accent, "your days of spreading foul breath are numbered!"

The accent was so bad it rivaled Ben Affleck's in *Shakespeare in Love*. The director, who I later learned had been making television commercials for the better part of thirty years, threw up his hands.

"All right, cut! Louie, you know I love ya, but I need you to lose the accent."

"Come on, Jeff. Let me do one more. I swear, I can get it to sound like Benedict Cumberbatch."

"No! Look, we've done eleven takes already, and I am way behind." He checked his watch. "Do it straight so we can all go home to our families, 'kay?"

"I haven't been to one of my kid's baseball games in, like, forever," the AD said.

Still looking at Louie, the director pointed to the AD. "See?"

"Aw, man... Come on. I did *Camelot* at the Cerritos Center!"

"And it stunk up the room," one of the grips said to us, his voice barely a whisper.

Dad shook his head and touched Matt's shoulder. "This guy can't play Sam. He's an idiot."

Phoebe sucked in air through her teeth. She looked like she wanted to upchuck. I was hoping it was something she ate.

"He's been trying forever to break into features," she said. "Besides, he'll work for free."

"Free doesn't mean good, Phoebe."

"Also, women love him," Matt said. "Date movie, remember?"

Twenty minutes later, the director called it a wrap. I didn't think what they'd gotten was all that good, but I supposed it was fine for a commercial. The four of us walked out with Louie and headed a little ways west on Melrose to Lucy's, which was almost directly across from that famous gate at Paramount Pictures. I overheard the actor telling Phoebe and Matt he'd recently auditioned for *Roadside Hospital*.

"I didn't think that thing was still in production," Matt said.

"Oh yeah, they're going on forty years."

"So, what's the part?"

"I'd be playing the doctor of a young female coma patient. Dr. St. Claire."

"Didn't Austin St. Claire die?" Phoebe said.

"Apparently, this is his son, Brahms."

"Ahh. What happened to the girl?"

"Head trauma, I think."

Once inside the restaurant, we sat in a booth and waited as Louie flipped through Dad's screenplay.

"So, you want me to be Sam. He's the hero?"

"Yes!" Matt said.

Phoebe broke in. "Actually..."

"It's not that kind of movie," Dad said. "It's more of a romantic comedy. Right, guys?"

Phoebe nodded quickly. "We want you because we need someone who's ripped."

"Yeah, that's good," Louie said. "Can I do it with a British accent?"

"No!" everyone said, almost causing the server passing us to drop a steaming platter of chicken fajitas.

"What we mean is," Dad said, "he's from LA, so."

"Oh, that's too bad."

"He's really ripped, though," Phoebe said.

Matt agreed, stuffing his face with tortilla chips. "Huge."

Louie flipped through the rest of the script, then put it down. "I'll do it."

"Great!" Phoebe said.

He leaned over and spoke to Matt confidentially. "Do you think I could get paid this time?"

"Louie, you always ask me that."

"My agent makes me. Hey, who's playing Kate?"

Phoebe's face lost its color. "We don't... I mean, we haven't—"

"For a minute, I thought you were gonna say Tara." He let out a horselaugh and tried the salsa.

Phoebe and Matt laughed along with him, and I figured it was a private joke. On an impulse, Dad handed his phone to our waiter, who took our picture. Louie held up the screenplay, one corner of which was bright red with what appeared to be blood but was actually salsa. Phoebe was faking a smile pretty badly, and I had the feeling there was something about this thing that wasn't quite kosher.

12

"You want to eat the writer? Be my guest. That will leave *you* to explain how else your character is supposed to get to Bremen!"

— SHADOW OF THE VAMPIRE

I am no expert, but here is what I know about the Pink School. It was old and very charming, like Picfair back in the day. It had originally been founded in the late 1800s as Jericho College, a Christian school for men, and was situated in the green, rolling hills of Malibu. By 1960, the school had gone coed, which some might have considered strange since Woodstock hadn't even happened yet.

In 1969, the great-granddaughter of the school's founder was discovered brutally murdered on the school grounds. At the time, it was thought she'd been killed by the Manson family prior to their later, more infamous bloodbath in Benedict Canyon. But nothing was ever proved. Shortly after, the school closed its doors for good.

In 1972, Harvey Pink, financed by a group of real estate

investors, purchased the property, believing he could convert the thing into—get this—a *movie studio*. Apparently, Roger Corman was Pink's idol, and the ex-fur salesman from New York went out and bought used cameras, and sound and lighting equipment, as well as old props and costumes. They reopened under the name American Worldwide Pictures, with a slate of low-budget horror movies and angsty teen dramas à la *High School Confidential*. But Pink was never able to line up the necessary distribution and, anxious to cover his losses, he got the brilliant idea of converting the property into a film school. He hired has-been movie and television directors, writers, cinematographers, and editors as faculty at the newly christened Pink School. After miraculously making the school profitable, he paid back his investors in full.

As time went on, he modernized the facilities and hired better teachers. By 2000, the campus was state of the art and boasted six hundred students. Pink, himself a graduate of the eighth grade, was presented with an honorary doctorate from NYU, and died peacefully in his sleep in 2006, surrounded by his three ex-wives, eleven children, and thirty-four grandchildren.

Why am I telling you this? Because Phoebe, Matt, Dad, and I were sitting in a conference room at the Pink School, where a team of Hollywood hacks had once churned out the screenplay for *Creature from the Dark Swamp*. Today, Matt was wearing a tasteful black Borsalino fedora that I had to admit looked good on him. We were joined by several other film school students, each with a script of *Endless Honeymoon* in their sweaty little hands.

"So, Alan," Matt said. "This is some of our crew. We've got Eric, set designer; Bailey, script supervisor; Owen, transportation captain; Uri, our DP, of course; and Jade, our editor."

"I've already locked down most of the locations," Phoebe said. "The actors will wear their own clothes."

Matt snapped his fingers, which I could tell really irritated Phoebe. "Equipment?"

"I'm still trying to line up a high-def camera. Every one of the school's has been checked out by other productions. But we have everything else."

"Hang on," Dad said. "Let's go back to location. This story is supposed to take place in Hawaii. How can we afford to fly everyone over there?"

Matt had this incredible talent for being condescending even when sitting quietly, popping the cap of a red Sharpie on and off. This time was no exception.

"We'll be shooting at a B&B near Solvang," Phoebe said.

Dad gave me a worried look. "Solvang?"

I decided it was time to be part of the solution. "Dad, it's really pretty up there."

"I know, honey, but—"

"Uri is a fantastic DP," Matt said. "It'll be magical, you'll see."

Dad and I got a load of Uri, who resembled a millennial Rasputin, except for the nasty Doritos crumbs in his ginger beard.

"Piss of cake," Uri said.

Dad smiled at me through clenched teeth. "Great."

"Am I late?" someone said.

We turned to find an attractive Indian woman at the door. She looked like she was around thirty, with these flashing brown eyes. I'm not usually psychic, but I would have bet my 1955 Dell First Edition copy of *The Body*

Snatchers that she had a whale of a temper. She approached Dad and shook his hand.

"Alan? Tara Singh."

"Her real name is Mugdha," Owen said to me in a low voice. "She changed it when she came to LA."

Tara was, what is the word, *bubbly*? And very self-aware. I kept expecting her to ask if we were being filmed.

"I love your script. I'm going to relish playing Kate."

Relish? Who did she think she was, the Dowager Countess of Grantham?

Phoebe choked on her own saliva. "Tara has been in nearly every student film for the past eight—"

"Nine," Tara said.

"Years."

"Yeah, she's kind of an institution around here," Matt said, wiggling his eyebrows at me under his hat.

Owen leaned over. "If you like buildings with asbestos."

"I'm very happy to meet you," Dad said. "You know, you remind me of Kareena Kapoor."

Okay, how does he do that? Tara took his arm and smiled, showing off her pearly whites, which creeped me out, since there was an itsy-bitsy speck of cilantro stuck in one of the crevices.

"How cute are you?" she said.

"Oh, and this is my daughter, Ruby."

"Hi," I said, extending my hand professionally.

"Matt, I need to run," Tara said, ignoring me. "I just wanted to stop by to meet everyone." She got as far as the door, then, "Oh, I meant to ask. Who's playing Sam?"

Everyone but Dad and me averted their eyes. Even Owen wasn't making eye contact. Matt pulled on his ear while Phoebe pretended she had received an important text.

"We, uh, haven't really..." Matt said.

Dad leaned in. "What're you talking about?"

Out of the corner of my eye, I could see Phoebe waving her hands, trying to get Dad's attention.

"It's that guy, what's-his-head. Louie something. Pacino... DiCaprio... No, that's not right."

Tara's expression got scary all of a sudden. I could feel the room shrinking as the oxygen was slowly sucked out.

"De Niro?" she said, her left eye twitching violently.

"Yeah, that's the guy!" Dad said, laughing and trying to high-five me. "He's not bad looking. I think he'll make a great Sam. I didn't think so at first, but now—"

Tara directed her fury at Matt. "Is this a joke?"

I swear, her voice had gone up at least an octave and sounded like a dentist's drill. Bailey and Jade covered their ears.

"I don't understand," Dad said.

He turned to his brother for help. Phoebe shook her head slowly and cleared her throat. When she spoke, we could barely hear her.

"She and Louie, well. They kind of don't get along. At all. Ever."

Tara was breathing fire. "I'd like to throw him into the wood chipper!"

Louie's earlier comment made sense to me now. These two had a bad history. A long, awkward silence hung in the room. The others pretended to reread the screenplay. I had never witnessed a real standoff and wondered what Matt would do. He folded his hands in front of him and cleared his throat.

"I guess you can't have the part then, Tara. Because we're going with Louie."

When I first laid eyes on this woman, I thought she was pretty scary. I mean, I could have easily pictured her summoning Shiva to, I don't know, *destroy the world?* She stood there, defiant, staring into Matt's soul. Then, I started doing it. And what I saw there was a cold, dark place that made me shiver.

"Hey. I'm a professional, right?" Tara said, her voice returning to a normal range.

"With no agent."

Owen had said that loud enough for Tara to hear. As the other students giggled, she shot them a look that would melt pig iron.

"See you on set!" she said, smiling coldly. Then to me, "It was nice meeting you, Trudy."

Dad and I waved weakly as she left the room, her over-sized Coach bag almost taking Phoebe's head off. Everyone in the room relaxed, except for Dad. He sat there, twiddling his thumbs and staring at an invisible black hole in the middle of the table.

"So, Matt, let me get this straight," he said. "We're making a love story—the love story of the century—the story that's going to help me get Stacey back. *And they hate each other's guts?*"

"Well, you know," Phoebe said, "when Cary Grant and Sophia Loren made *Houseboat*—"

"Not helping, Phoebe!" Dad said.

"Sorry."

Putting on his *Okay, we'll throw in the floor mats for free* smile, he said to the other students, "Why don't you guys Snapchat or something?"

They couldn't get out of there fast enough. As the last of them ran out, Dad turned to Phoebe.

"I'm the producer, remember?"

He got up and closed the door, then walked around the table slowly, like Robert De Niro in *The Untouchables*. "Guys, this whole thing is a little loosey-goosey. I don't think you two fully appreciate what's riding on this."

"Alan, I know how you feel," Matt said. "But this is the way it works. I mean, there's always gonna be glitches. Did you ever read Edith Blake's book about the making of *Jaws*?"

"For crying out loud, Matt, you know I didn't!"

"'Strangely enough, it all turns out well.'"

"Now you're quoting *Shakespeare in Love* to me? All right, I admit this isn't my world. But I've been in business a long time, Matt. And there's something... Something's not copacetic about this whole operation. For example, what about the crew? You've got, what, five people? And the cast. I've only seen two actors. Who's going to play the kindly old couple who own the beach house?"

"Oh, you mean the caretaker and his wife," Matt said.

"What?" Dad was clearly in over his head, and we hadn't even started principal photography. "So, have you found someone?"

"We've got these two veteran actors," Phoebe said, glancing at Matt for confirmation. "We're finalizing things as we speak."

Dad wasn't convinced. "What about the other speaking parts? And the locations?"

"Alan, we have it under control," Matt said. "This is what we do."

Dad got quiet. He rubbed his eyes and cleared his throat like he was holding back a tsunami of tears and memories. And it was starting to affect Phoebe, for some reason.

"Matt, listen to me," he said. "Stacey is about to marry some rich guy who, obviously, I can't compete with. He's planning to make a life with her and Ruby." He took my hand and smiled sadly. "And I can't let that happen.

"I thought if I could make this movie, she'd see how

much love there is between us, for better or worse. I want you to promise me this will work."

Choking back a sob, Phoebe got up and ran out of the room. What was up with her, anyways?

"Sorry, she gets emotional sometimes," Matt said. "Look, this is gonna be a film you can be proud of. Okay, big bro?"

"Sure," Dad said.

But something about the way Phoebe had reacted to Dad's confession bothered me on a very deep level.

LATER, outside in the corridor, Phoebe sat slumped against the wall, crying as Matt held her by the shoulders. The afternoon light shining through the tall windows cast stark shadows everywhere. Alan and Ruby had already gone home. And there was no one else around.

"This is gonna work out," Matt said. "You'll see."

He handed Phoebe some coarse paper towels he had gotten from the men's restroom and waited while she blew her nose.

"But Alan has no clue, Matt. What happens when..."

"This is our dream, remember?"

Phoebe didn't answer. She wondered if continual violent cramping could eventually lead to stomach cancer, and made a mental note to look it up on WebMD later.

13

"Look, you ever read that book *She's Just Not That into You*?"

— Zombieland

The *Texas Chain Saw Massacre* and *Halloween*—both horror classics—did nothing to brighten my spirits. I was certifiably depressed as Claire, Diego, and I walked out of the Nuart Theatre onto Santa Monica Boulevard. I looked up at the marquee displaying the gruesome double bill and sighed, thinking back to my childhood when I used to love this stuff.

"You hungry?" Diego said.

I looked at him miserably. "I guess."

"Souplantation?" Claire said.

"Claire, everybody knows 'buffet' is French for 'shovel.'"

"Wow, you *are* in a bad mood."

Diego smiled hopefully. "Hole in the Wall?"

I shrugged. Come to think of it, maybe a nice hunk of rare red meat would cheer me up. As we walked east, I thought about a low-budget rom-com actually getting Mom and Dad back together. It was ridiculous. Not to mention, I was still feeling queasy about the whole Matt thing. I knew there was something he wasn't telling us. I could feel it. And Phoebe! I mean, what was the deal with her? On the other hand, I could've imagined the whole thing. Wouldn't be the first time. Anyways, I wasn't feeling good about things in general, hence my mood.

"It's never going to work," I said after we'd walked under the freeway overpass. "My family is doomed."

Diego stopped me. "You got to think positive, girl."

"I don't want an absent father, okay?"

Great. I had yelled at one of my closest friends. I needed to snap out of it.

"Sorry, Diego. I know you're only trying to help."

"And besides," Claire said, "there's always hope."

Diego went on as if nothing had happened, and in my heart, I thanked him for letting me slide.

"Here's what I think," he said. "You should talk to your mom. When my family was going through all that *pedo* before, it's something I never did. I kept everything to myself."

"Your parents didn't know how you felt about the split?" Claire said.

"I never said anything. I thought I was being, you know, macho. Maybe if I'd spoken up."

I sighed again. "It's like I'm trying to hold back a tidal wave."

"Of *caca*," Diego said.

Claire joined in. "With an umbrella."

"In your chonies."

Claire laughed. "On Halloween."

"Oh!" I said. "Would you two stop? This is not even funny."

In spite of myself, I was giggling. Diego took my hand, which I thought was strange, since he'd never tried doing that before.

"I'm glad we're friends," I said, taking my hand back and giving Claire a WTF look.

Diego stuck his hands in his pockets. "Yeah, friends. That's cool."

Claire and I watched as he walked ahead.

When we got to the restaurant, I said to Diego, "What time's your mom picking us up?"

"Five."

"Then, I guess we'll have time for chocolate chip cookies after."

I was starting to feel a tiny bit better. It was probably the burger. Claire and I talked nonstop about books, movies, and the cute clothes we wanted to buy at Topshop. I couldn't help but notice, though, that Diego had gone quiet. Maybe those movies had gotten to him. Understandable. He wasn't a horror veteran like Claire and me.

Yeah, that must've been it—the movies.

DIEGO RIVERA SAT at the kitchen table, drinking chocolate milk and playing *Minecraft* on his phone. An only child, he sometimes longed to have an older brother he could talk to. His dad wasn't around all the time, and there was no other male in his life. His mom had always tried to be understanding, but she knew nothing about teenage boys. Then again, she might surprise him. As she stood behind him preparing enchiladas to go into the oven, he decided to give it a try.

"Ma?"

"*Mande.*"

"What do you do when you have a friend you really care about, but you don't wanna be friends anymore?"

"We're talking about a girl?"

"Ma... Yes, a girl."

"You mean Ruby."

"Yeah."

"*Pues*, she's a smart girl, but I could do without *los monstruos.*"

"At least she's not goth."

"That's something."

She slipped the Pyrex baking dish into the oven, set the timer, and joined her son at the table.

"You don't wanna be friends?" she said.

"I think I want something else."

"Oh."

"Today, I took her hand and she got all weird about it."

"That means she's not ready."

"What am I supposed to do? What if she's never ready?"

"Going from friend to boyfriend is a one-way trip, *mijo.*"

"What does that mean?"

"It means if things don't work out, you've lost a girlfriend *and* a friend."

"*Mierda*, I never thought of that."

"Watch your mouth. It doesn't mean you shouldn't try, Diego. But you might lose her."

"So, what should I do?"

She patted his hand and got up. "I have to make a salad."

"Ma, what do I do?"

She stroked his cheek. "Give her time."

"That's it? That's your advice?"

"*Si tu mal tiene remedio, ¿de qué te apuras? Y si no, ¿de qué te preocupas?*"

For a long time, Diego sat there thinking about what his mother had said. *If there's a cure for your problem, why anguish? And if there's no cure, why worry?* What if there *was* no cure? The last thing he wanted was to ruin what Ruby and he had. He was so confused. One day they were best friends, hanging out and doing normal friend stuff. But now, suddenly, she was a *girl*. A funny, crazy, smart, meat-eating, machinima-making, horror-loving girl who was hella cute. When did that happen? She was all he could think about. Sighing, he decided to take his mom's advice and give Ruby some time. What else could he do when friendship was on the line?

RUBY HERE. It wasn't like me to spy on people, but these were troubling times. I didn't know what my mother was up to, and I needed to talk to her before things went any farther. Claire had said there was always hope. Bless her heart. I was more of a pessimist. And Diego. What in the world was up with that boy? He'd been acting weird around me for days. Was he having problems at home, too? Never mind. I needed to concentrate on the task at hand. Time to go all ninja!

I had never been to the City Club, which was located in downtown LA. Instead of catching a bus, I Ubered it to Bunker Hill. The driver was nice. College kid. Originally from Alabama. I fought the urge to answer his routine questions using movie quotes from *Talladega Nights*. Where was I? The Arbor Room was packed. Nothing but well-dressed business types drinking dirty martinis and stuff. I had talked my way in, telling the maître d' I was meeting my mom and that it was supposed to be a surprise. To my amazement, he bought it. Sucker.

Mom was sitting with that creep Warren Mudge at a romantic table near a window that overlooked LA, and he was stroking her fingers—ew! I hid behind a dessert cart to do a little Observe & Report.

"When I didn't see you wearing the ring, I was prepared to go out the window," Warren said.

He was one of those people who laughed at their own jokes. For the record, I hate that. Anyways, Mom did not look happy. Why was she even here?

"I've been thinking a lot about this, Warren," she said. "But there's Ruby to consider. I want what's best for her."

"Understood."

Even when this guy pretended to be human, he was disturbing. Sort of like Oscar Isaac in *Ex Machina*.

"And it's how I hoped you'd feel," he said. "Putting the children first, which is exactly what I want."

I couldn't take it anymore. I popped out like a jack-in-the-box, almost tipping over the cart. Go, ninjas!

"Speaking of children," I said.

Mom gawped at me and quickly put her hands in her lap. Warren sat there with his hands pressed together, a strange little smile on his face. Something told me he liked drama.

"Ruby, what're you doing here?" Mom said.

"Your assistant told me where you were."

"Where's your father?"

"He thinks I'm at Claire's."

"It's good to see you again, Ruby," Warren said, getting up and pulling out a chair for me. "You've certainly grown since—"

"Put a sock in it, Warren."

I'm not a rude person, but this guy was getting on my last nerve.

"Ruby!" Mom said. Then to Warren, "I'm so sorry. She's not usually like this."

The little creep grabbed his phone and smiled like Pennywise.

"I need to catch up on some e-mails," he said. "I'll talk to you tomorrow, Stacey. Don't worry about the bill. I'll tell them to charge it to my account."

He folded his napkin and left it on his chair while Mom continued glaring at me. I knew I was in for it.

"Sorry about dinner," she said.

He stood directly in front of me. Honestly, I thought he was about to use the stolen Elder Wand. I realized he and I were almost the same height, and I had to concentrate on a salad fork that had fallen on the floor to keep myself from grinning.

"Ruby."

Yes, Voldemort?

"I'm not the bad guy. I'm the *right* guy."

Oh, brother. I wanted to knee this guy right in his Dark Lord junk, and I could feel my cheeks getting hot. Once he was gone I brushed his napkin away like it was toxic and plopped myself down. Mom was still livid. She scooted her chair closer. Then, came the pointing finger. Here we go.

"Now, you listen to me," she said. "You can't waltz in here and talk to my boss that way. Who do you think you are?"

"Whatev'," I said, buttering a slice of bread.

"What has gotten into you?"

I took a huge bite. "So are you marrying him?"

"Who told you— Your father..."

She looked like she wanted to scream. At this point, I

would've happily joined her. Taking a breath, she reached for my hand and gave me the saddest smile I've ever seen.

"Are you hungry?" she said.

After my Tournedos Rossini had arrived, Mom spent the whole time watching me chow down instead of eating her own pasta. For a time, I pretended I was alone and concentrated on the food. I could hardly taste anything, though. Guilt will do that.

"I knew it, your father is starving you to death," she said.

"Look, he feeds me, okay?"

"Ruby, why did you come here tonight?"

I didn't answer her. As I picked at my veggies, Mom grabbed her phone and fired up her annoying translation app. Then, repeating the question, she held the phone up to my face.

"*¿Por qué has venido aquí esta noche?*" the app said. I was silent as the grave. "*Pourquoi êtes-vous venu ici ce soir?*"

"I can do this all night," she said. "Let's see, I think I'll try Esperanto."

"Stop it," I said, giggling. "This is hard for me."

"I'm listening."

"I guess it's... I always thought somehow you and Dad would be getting back together at some point. That you'd work out whatever it was made you guys split up in the first place." No reaction—I panicked. "Unless it was me!"

Mom shook her head and looked away. "You know, there are so many things I regret."

"So, it *was* me?"

I wanted to die. Maybe if I'd been more like Evelyn Dubicki, who sold Girl Scout cookies, loved camping, and whose favorite band was One Direction—before the whole Zayn Malik kerfuffle.

"No, sweetie," she said. "You are the most important

thing to your father and me. But we were both working professionals, and we wanted to provide you with everything we were capable of.

"There were so many times I wanted to quit and be with you when you were growing up. But your father would always talk me out of it. 'How will we live? What about her college?'

"His mother was never around either because she worked. It was all he knew. And I suppose I bought into it, too."

Whew! I felt a thousand pounds lighter. As if to help me celebrate *not* being a strange, unwanted child, a nice server placed a strawberry-rhubarb tart with a side of vanilla ice cream in front of me. I dug in.

"So why didn't you stay together?" I said. "I was fine with the way things were." *Ow, ow, ow! Brain freeze!*

"I know you were. Which is what made it worse. You never complained. The day care, the sitters..."

"So why, Mom? I need to know."

"Because I wanted another baby. Only this time I wanted to raise her myself. As usual, your father tried talking me out of it. It went from being a discussion to a fight. Then, he gave away your crib without telling me. That hurt me so much. It was like he didn't respect me. After that, we couldn't even be in the same room."

"I remember," I said. "Things were pretty tense back then. And you still want a baby?" Mom nodded. "Only... Warren would be the father? Would I still live with you?"

I wasn't hungry anymore and put my dessert fork down. Mom was crying. I didn't know what to do.

"I wouldn't want you to be anywhere else," she said.

Waterworks are very contagious, let me tell you. She opened her arms to me, and I went to her the way I used to when I was two, trying very hard not to lose my dignity completely. Mom's phone rang. She looked down at the number, and while kissing me and wiping her eyes, she answered it.

"Hi, Alan. No, I'm— Yes, she's here with me. She's fine. I'll bring her over later. Bye."

Outside the Museum of Contemporary Art, which was near the City Club, Mom sat on the edge of the fountain as I took video of her with my camcorder.

"How did you and Dad meet?" I said.

"Ruby, you already know this story."

"Tell it to the camera."

I could see these were pleasant memories, and as Mom smiled into the camera, I tried framing the shot a little tighter. I wished I had better lighting.

"I remember I had just gotten my first real job. My dad wanted me to have a good car and offered to pay. I did my research and decided on a Lexus. It was your father who sold it to me. After that, we started dating. Six months later, we were engaged. Then, we got married, and a year later, you were born."

"Were you happy?"

"Ecstatic."

"Are you happy now?"

"Sweetie, we need to go."

14

I could feel a lecture coming as Mom pulled her Lexus
ES up in front of Dad's apartment building. She
turned off the engine and looked at me with a serious
expression.

"Ruby, you have to promise me you won't wander off like
that again."

Oh no, not the little finger! I rolled my eyes, but Mom
persisted. Slowly, I extended my little finger, too, and pinky-
promised her. I prayed no one was watching us.

"I promise," I said and unbuckled my seatbelt. "Mom?
Dad and I are going up to Solvang for a few days. I didn't
want you to worry."

"Why didn't he tell me himself?"

"I'm sure he's planning to."

"How are things with him?"

"Okay...I guess."

"Is he seeing anyone?"

"Mom!"

"He wasn't too happy the last time we were together."

"You could cheer him up now," I said.

"What? No, I don't think so."

"Come on, just for a minute."

I practically catapulted out of the car, ran around to the other side, and dragged her out.

"Ruby, this isn't a good idea."

"It's a fantastic idea!" I said.

I yanked the keys from the ignition and ran toward the front entrance, dangling them in the air. Then, I tried out my evil laugh. Never mind, that needed some work.

"You're not leaving here until you come in!" I said.

A couple of minutes later, Mom was sitting on a bar stool in the kitchen as Dad pretended to putter. She and I both knew he was nervous because he never puttered. Sure, sometimes he would procrastinate—and once he'd even prevaricated—but the man *never* puttered.

Since she arrived, Ed had stayed close to Mom. I kissed each of my parents dramatically and disappeared, intending to leave my bedroom door open so I wouldn't miss anything.

"Going to my room! Come on, Ed." The dog ignored me.

"I already yelled at her for running away," Mom said.

Judging by her tone, I didn't think she was all that angry. Maybe she *had* wanted to be here and needed an excuse? After what seemed like minutes, Dad finally spoke up.

"Want some coffee?"

Silence. I couldn't understand why no one was saying anything. When the coffee was ready, they moved to the living room. Dad put on a John Coltrane ballad to set the mood. I'm pretty sure it was "You Don't Know What Love Is." He was old school and only owned vinyl. For years, he had tried to convert me. As a result, I had practically memorized his entire jazz collection.

"The music's great," Mom said. "I really miss it."

"You don't listen to jazz anymore?"

"No." She forced a laugh. "Someone heard I liked it and gave me a smooth jazz CD for Christmas."

"Ouch."

"Don't worry, I regifted it."

"Who else do you hate that much, besides me?"

She laughed, this time for realz. "I don't hate you, Alan. And, if you must know, I donated it to the library."

Though it sounded like things were on track, I wanted to see for myself. So I sneaked into the hallway and stayed glued to the wall, watching my parents *not* being romantic.

"You still have the old turntable?" he said.

Dad thumbed through his collection, grabbed an album, and handed it to Mom. Though I saw the cover only briefly, I knew it was Chet Baker's "Lonely Star." Wow, I never thought he would part with that!

"What? No," she said.

"Take it."

"Alan, no. You love Chet Baker. I remember the first time you played 'Serenity' for me. I couldn't."

"I want you to have it, Stace. Please. The thought of you not having any real jazz in the house is more than I can bear."

"That's sweet. Thank you."

She laid the album next to her purse. A long, awkward silence filled the space between them. Well, at least they were in the same room together.

"Ruby said you two are driving up to Solvang?" Mom said. "Don't tell me you're finally taking a vacation."

I realized I hadn't warned Dad and wondered if he would be able to improv. Then, I remembered—he was a salesman.

"Yeah, I thought she and I needed some time away from the city."

Nice one, Alan. Come on, get to the smooching already.

"I think she'll like that," Mom said. "Want me to take Ed?"

"That would be great, thanks." He gave her a warm-up and refilled his own cup. "Don't worry, it's decaf."

Mom wandered around the living room, holding her coffee and checking out the decor. I had never understood that metaphor about an elephant in the room. But I could almost picture the beast as Mom made her way around it.

"You did a nice job of decorating the place," she said.

"You can thank IKEA."

Dad watched her as she held a photograph of the three of us in happier times. That particular pic occupied a special place on the mantle, next to Dad's prized baseball bobblehead collection. It was taken after I had lost my first tooth. We'd gone to Disneyland, and I was grinning into the camera in front of Pirates of the Caribbean with this huge hole in my teeth.

"Listen, Stace," Dad said. "I may have overreacted at lunch the other day, and I owe you a steak. I'm really sorry."

"No, it's understandable." She was still looking at the photograph. "I didn't give you much warning."

She put the photo back and took in the rest of the room. I hoped they would get down to business.

"This is not easy for me," she said. "I can't imagine this past year has been easy for you either. Not seeing your daughter every day. I want you to know that whatever my decision, I'm putting Ruby first."

Dad looked at his wedding ring. Mom had put hers away months ago.

"Are you?" he said. "What I mean is, if you were putting her first, wouldn't you stop this nonsense and let us be a family again?"

Uh-oh, this couldn't be good. Abort! Abort!

"*Nonsense?* Is that what you think it is? Alan, do you even know what this is about?"

"Sure. It's about you wanting another baby to lessen your 'guilt' over not staying home with Ruby."

"I don't believe this. It has nothing to do with guilt. It's about wanting a better life! That's not guilt. And don't ever use air quotes with me again."

"It *is* guilt, Stace."

"You're an idiot, you know that?"

"Oh, *I'm* an idiot? You didn't *do* anything to her, Stacey. Look at her. She's fine!"

"This is not about Ruby. You never wanted me to stay home because your mother never did!"

"My mother did what she had to, under the circumstances."

"And by the looks of it, she did a bang-up job. Maybe I *should* marry Warren and leave you to wallow in your blissful childhood memories of being a latchkey kid. I'm sure there are women out there dying to hear your lurid stories about drinking milk from the carton."

"Oh, don't worry about me, baby. I've had plenty of offers!"

"That's right. I forgot about Mrs. Tannenbaum down the hall."

"It's *Tessenbaum*. And at least she knows a good man when she sees one!"

Mom grabbed Dad's cup and shrieked into it, startling the dog and making him bark.

"What was that?" he said.

"It's the scream in your coffee."

This had not gone the way I'd hoped. I beat it back to my room and, tripping over my duffel bag, took a major flyer onto the carpet.

"I'm okay!" I said.

The two of them were too engrossed in their problems to notice that I'd almost broken my nose. What I heard next were keys jingling, followed by the front door slamming, and finally, the door opening again.

"I forgot the dog," Mom said.

Soon, she was off again. I collapsed onto my bed and beat my temples with my fists.

"Oh! I don't believe it! They're both insane!"

Later, I sat in front of my laptop, watching as my machinima movie came to life by itself. The scene was the City Club. Mom and Warren were locked in a pukey embrace at a table by the window. Outside, the sky was in flames.

"Yes, Warren," Machinima Mom said in a creepy metallic voice. "I *will* marry you!"

"My darling!" Machinima Warren said, his voice also metallic.

They kissed mechanically as the scene dissolved into a close-up of a red velvet theater curtain. A claw-like hand pulled back the curtain, and a shadowy face appeared, hidden by a high-crown hat. It was my machinima killer.

"Something must be done," he said.

The scene shifted to the wet nighttime streets of WeHo

—and *I* was there, walking Ed. The night was moonless. Ahead of me, I saw Mrs. Tessenbaum walking her Yorkshire terrier. She stopped and looked at me. Giving me an odd smile, she disappeared around a corner. Ed barked like a maniac and dragged me on.

When we turned the corner, the old lady was gone, and Warren Mudge was walking the dog. Cold sweat beaded on his forehead. Out of nowhere, a fleet of garbage trucks rumbled past, blocking my view. Ed and I waited.

After the trucks were gone, I saw Rick Van Loon holding the leash. He glanced over his shoulder, so I hid behind a recycling bin. I watched as he stopped near a hedge. There wasn't a car in sight as the dog sniffed around. I heard something that sounded like a faraway laugh. Rick looked up.

My killer, wearing his hat and duster, was grinning at him. Rick—who had become Warren again—screamed insanely, but the noise from the chainsaw drowned him out. Shutting my eyes, I could hear the sound of flesh tearing. Then, all was quiet. I cracked one eye open and saw the Yorkie running toward us, yapping furiously and dragging his leash.

The hand was still attached.

When I opened my eyes, I realized I had fallen asleep on top of my bed, still in my clothes. The stain on the ceiling had morphed into a full-out rendering of the killer in grays and blacks. I thought he might be trying to tell me something. I looked at Mr. Shivers, preparing myself for the inevitable comeback. Slowly, the doll turned its head and said something I never expected.

"'They're coming to get you, Barbara.'"

SHRIEKING, I sat straight up and, seeing my laptop in front of me at my desk, finally figured out I had actually been asleep *the whole time*. Whew! And for the record? I am not a fan of the whole "dream within a dream" trope. Just sayin'.

15

"These are godless times, Mrs. Snell."

— CARRIE (1976)

S tacey raced up Mandeville Canyon Road, gripping the wheel hard to keep herself from screaming. It was dark, and she wasn't negotiating the curves very well. The street was mostly deserted, except for a few stragglers returning home from late-night doings. Nocturnal creatures crossing the road were common, she remembered. *Slow down, Stacey!*

"That *jerk!*" she said to Ed, who was cowering in the backseat. "What does he know about guilt? This is what I get for being honest."

Knowing she would end up there, yet choosing to ignore the glaring truth of her own desperate actions, she found herself in front of Warren's house, a mini-mansion located on a tiny piece of property on top of a hill. The white two-story home done in a faux Neoclassical style that Stacey hated gleamed spookily in the moonlight, reminding her of a haunted funeral home she'd seen once in a horror movie. She stopped abruptly in the driveway and, after checking on the dog, ran breathlessly toward the front door. When she rang the bell, the chimes echoed eerily inside. No one answered. She tried again and stepped back, gazing up at the curved balcony.

"What am I doing?" she said.

The white shuttered doors were open. A soft night breeze made the sheer curtains move in and out like slow, phantasmal breathing. Eventually, Warren appeared on the balcony in blue jeans, barefoot and shirtless, his hair in disarray.

"Stacey? What—"

"You were right, Warren," she said. "It's time to act."

His eyes shifted nervously. Not exactly the reaction she was hoping for. Clearly, this had been a mistake.

"Can we discuss it tomorrow?" he said.

She didn't understand. She was sure he would be thrilled to see her, especially after the fiasco at the City Club. But something was wrong. Her throat became tight, and then, she knew.

"Is someone in there with you?" she said.

He didn't answer for a long time. "Yes."

Even from up there he could see the disappointment in her face. He watched as she marched back to her car.

"Look, I'm not a monk!" he said. "I promise, this ends after we're married."

"Warren?" a woman's voice said from inside.

"Stacey, wait!"

She had started the engine and was pulling away when a loud thud on her roof startled her. Warren's head appeared upside down on the windshield, and Stacey screamed. Ed went wild, alternately barking and snarling.

"Stop the car!" Warren said.

Adrenaline pumping through her veins, she floored it and careened down the steep, winding road as Warren clung to the windshield wipers.

"Get off!"

"Can't we talk about this?" he said.

She refused to look at him, even though his eyes were bugging out and his flailing feet came within inches of the mailboxes flying past.

Raccoons!

Stacey swerved violently and hit the brakes. The car screeched sideways to a stop and nearly tipped over, and the smell of burning rubber singed her nostrils. Warren flew off the roof wildly and over a steep embankment. Having been in business a long time, Stacey thought she knew every possible reason why a person might be fired. She had to admit, this was a first. Gathering her strength, she checked on the dog again, then got out and peered down into the darkness of the ravine below.

"Oh, hell," she said, her mouth tasting of metal. "Warren?"

AT THE HOSPITAL, Warren Mudge lay battered, bruised, and barely conscious on the emergency room table as a young doctor finished his examination. Stacey watched from a few feet away, numb, chewing the nail of her thumb. When she thought about returning the ring, she realized she was relieved. She had never wanted to marry her boss. Too bad it took almost killing him for her to come to her senses.

"Mrs. Mudge?" the doctor said.

"No, I'm not—I just work for him."

"Oh, sorry. As you can see, he's pretty banged up. He's lucky he keeps himself in good physical condition. From what I've been able to determine so far, he has a broken arm and some cracked ribs. There could be some spinal damage."

"When will you know?"

"I'll need to see the X-rays. I'm hoping there isn't any organ damage or internal bleeding. I'd like to keep him under observation for a day or two."

"Sure," she said.

"What happened tonight?"

"It was an accident. He fell off the balcony."

Slowly, she turned and wandered out, wondering vaguely if she would be hearing from Warren's attorneys.

IN THE DARKNESS, Stacey sat at her kitchen table in a sad stupor, feeling as if a great weight had been lifted from her shoulders. How could she have been so wrong about her feelings? Normally, she was very sensible and knew exactly what she wanted, but lately, everything confused her. Under the circumstances, it might be best if she never remarried. She could focus all her attention on raising Ruby. After that, she might enter a convent.

When her phone vibrated again, she didn't move to answer it. Then, the home phone rang. Her arms felt so heavy. Without energy, she got to her feet and picked up the handset. A man's voice that sounded drugged was already pleading with her. If she'd had the strength, she would have ripped the cord out of the wall.

"I can't talk about this now, Warren," she said. "I know

you're not a monk. Look, will you— I need time to work this out. Sorry you got hurt."

She hung up and noticed her purse sitting on the table next to the record album Alan had given her. She thought about a particular night five years earlier.

It was the weekend. She had been straightening up the home office. Alan was busy editing old videos and not paying any attention to her.

"I wish *I* had time to play on the computer."

"This is going to be great, you'll see," he said, unaware there was a problem.

"Can't you at least try to keep this room clean? You're in here more than I am."

He touched her hand. "Hey, come on, Stace."

She was feeling sulky and doodled on his back as he sat and worked.

"I want to try again," she said. "Can we try again?"

"I'm happy to," he said, concentrating on the monitor.

"And this time I want to stay home."

He stopped and looked at her. "Stace, I want another baby, too, but—"

"You have to work, honey," she said, trying to sound like her husband.

Ruby, now nine, marched in, carrying a lump of metal with wires, followed by the puppy version of Ed. Both parents heard the *ka-ching* of the cash register at the same time.

"I need a new hard drive," Ruby said. "This one's toast."

Alan sighed. "We'll go on the weekend."

"Thanks, Dad. Hi, Mom."

She picked up the dog and left before Stacey could say anything.

"Hey, come here," Alan said.

He played her a clip of himself in the living room dancing with a four-year-old Ruby standing on his feet. They twirled to the music of Sinatra singing "Come Fly With Me" as the unseen Stacey laughed and tried her best not to shake the camera.

She hugged him gratefully. "I love you so much."

"We're calling that hard drive a birthday present," he said.

The living room was dark, and Stacey was alone, except for Ed, who was curled up on her lap. She had put on the record Alan gave her and was sitting on the floor in the moonlight that streamed through the windows as Chet Baker's sad ballad "Serenity" filled the air with a longing she never could have expressed in words.

16
___

"I'm scared to close my eyes. I'm scared to open them."

— THE BLAIR WITCH PROJECT

I t was evening when Phoebe parked on the cool, tree-lined street in Sherman Oaks. A dog yapped furiously as she trudged inescapably up a brick walkway toward the front door of a neatly manicured, recently landscaped suburban home. Her legs felt like cold lead, and she wished she could run. Slowly, she reached up to ring the bell, then chickened out and skittered away.

"This is insane," she said.

An owl sitting on the lowest branch of a eucalyptus tree stared down at her, his expression questioning her commitment to the project. Disgusted, she stuck her tongue out at it and forced herself to go back. As she stood on the porch, she took a manila envelope from her purse and counted the cash inside. It wasn't much—two hundred dollars in twenties. Insisting the bills be new, Matt had made her go to the bank. *What the hell, it might work.* Taking a breath, she pressed the doorbell and put on a plastic smile.

Inside, a two-tone chime rang pleasantly. The door opened, and a man who was very tall and appeared to have no politics waited for her to explain herself. Silently, she handed him the envelope.

"This is for Vicky," she said. "I called earlier?"

Before he could respond, she hurried away, tripping on a coiled garden hose. When she reached the sidewalk, she managed to stumble over a crate of recyclables sitting at the curb.

"Are you okay?" the man said.

"Outstanding." Her face hot, she walked fast toward her car.

THE DEN WAS TYPICAL, a semi-organized pastiche of books, board games, a flat screen TV, and an Xbox One. A generous collection of family pictures stood on the mantle, as well as the manila envelope Phoebe had left earlier that evening. Nadia sat opposite her spiritual advisor, a perky teenager named Vicky, who wore braces and favored pink fuzzy socks.

Vicky wasn't a spiritual advisor by trade. She was a bright, inquisitive high school honors student who read Kant and the New Testament and attended summer school at a local community college. And she was Ian's older sister. At dinner one night at her house, Nadia had realized the girl was extraordinarily gifted and found herself talking about things other than her little brother's dramatic skills, or lack thereof. After a while, Nadia would come to see her in times of great stress.

"They practically begged me to be in their film," Nadia said. "But I cannot."

"I remember you told me it was your dream to be up on the screen again," Vicky said, doodling on her yellow legal pad instead of taking notes.

"I have thought about it."

"Then, why not now? Because it would tear open old injuries?"

"Yes. I can't do it. I can't see Klaus again."

"Well, have you thought that maybe *he* wants to see *you*?"

Uncomfortable, Nadia looked away. The silence felt to her like late summer, still and dry.

Vicky scrunched her eyebrows together and tucked her tongue into the corner of her mouth, something she always did when confronted with a difficult math problem. She decided to try a different approach.

"What about forgiveness?"

"He would never forgive me," Nadia said, recognizing the bitterness in her own voice.

Vicky leaned forward, her child's eyes intensely kind. "I'm talking about *you* forgiving *yourself*, Nadia. You know? Sometimes it's okay to let yourself have what you really want."

How was it possible this young girl was so wise? Nadia had never told anyone the real story about what had happened all those years ago. She stared at Vicky, her eyes glistening. The girl handed her a box of tissues.

As Nadia blew her nose, Ian ran in. "Dad says to wind it up." Then, in his best Dad voice, "It's a school night, 'member?"

"Sorry," Vicky said to Nadia. "Big Psych test tomorrow."

She escorted Nadia out as the boy skipped ahead.

Holding the manila envelope, Vicky stood in the doorway with her client.

Nadia laughed self-consciously. "I'm so lost."

"I feel like you should do this movie," the girl said. "Or you'll never be at peace with yourself. Anyhoo—"

"Olly olly oxen free!" Ian said from somewhere inside the house.

"I have to go. Good night, Nadia."

Vicky handed her the unopened envelope and gently closed the door.

THE NEXT MORNING in her office at school, Nadia sat at her desk, her tea and a half-eaten Madeleine cookie in front of her. Phoebe waited with breathless expectation while Matt, wearing a navy Basque beret, fiddled with his phone. The old woman couldn't believe what she was doing, but would trust her spiritual advisor, who recently had managed to save her from making an ill-advised purchase at Lamps Plus.

"I've decided to do the film," Nadia said.

Matt looked up. "That's great."

"Thank you so much!" Phoebe said.

"But I require a vegan chef."

Phoebe pulled at her earlobe. "We can do Whole Foods, I guess."

"And a personal bodyguard on set at all times. There's no telling what that crazy German is capable of."

"Not a problem," Matt said.

As he and Phoebe got up to leave, he glanced nervously around the office. Then, he stuck his head out the open door.

"What're you doing?" Phoebe said.

The old woman smiled. "Ian is in acting class."

As Nadia saw them off, she handed Phoebe the manila envelope, the money still inside. Surprised, Phoebe accepted it.

"I believe this is yours," Nadia said. "I should have warned you, Vicky would never accept money for what she does. She considers it 'tacky.'"

"I am so sorry," Phoebe said, deeply embarrassed.

"Never mind. More money for Whole Foods." Smiling, she kissed the girl's cheek. "Next time, trust your own instincts."

"Yes, I will," Phoebe said, glaring at Matt.

THE RAIN CAME DOWN HARD like slanted blades as Sam and Kate slowly made their way through the thick, dangerous night in a midsize rental car. The windshield wipers barely worked, and Sam struggled to see where he was going. Kate turned and watched the caravan of cars behind them. They hit another pothole, jarring both of them to the bone.

"Man!" Sam said. "I've never even heard of the Black Hollow Inn."

"Sam, I know it's not where we wanted to stay, but it's still our honeymoon."

"I mean, what're the odds of our hotel burning down?"

She ran her hand seductively up the back of his neck, over his head, and onto his face. Gripping the wheel more tightly, he continued talking past her fingers.

"Kate, for crying out loud, let's not have an accident."

Gently, he pulled her hand away and fiddled with the

car radio. It was mostly static. He kept at it until he found a news station.

"...escaped killer is believed to be miles away from the asylum. Police are cautioning everyone to be on the lookout. He is extremely dangerous. And insane. Geiger Asylum officials offered no explanation—"

Sam switched off the radio and slowed down as they approached a lighted driveway. He wiped his hand across the fogged-up windshield.

"It doesn't look too bad," he said.

As the other cars parked next to one another, the caretaker and his wife watched stoically from the entrance. They were neither happy or sad, fearless or afraid. Only watchful.

Sam got the bags out of the trunk and approached the entrance with Kate. They were the first to reach the door.

"Hi," he said. "Our hotel burned down."

"Welcome to Black Hollow Inn," the caretaker's wife said, her voice cold and forbidding.

The caretaker grabbed the bags and disappeared inside. Carefully, Sam guided Kate past the disturbing woman. The other nervous guests followed saying nothing, in case she was on a hair trigger.

Their room was charming, if a little dated. As Kate unpacked, Sam sat on the edge of the bed, using a TV remote to bring up a channel—any channel. No luck. Everything was snow.

"Is not having a working TV going to be a problem?" she said.

"No, trying to get some scores, is all."

He snapped off the set, tossed the remote, and went to her. He kissed her tenderly. Somewhere a strange hissing noise interrupted them.

"Shame on me for thinking about professional sports," he said, getting into the mood.

"Who needs a professional when you can have an amateur?"

Annoyed, he looked away. "What is that noise?"

Uri was filming the scene while Phoebe, Matt, and Alan watched the video monitor. Matt had on a red Kangol cap turned backward—his "lucky" hat—which he would continue to wear exclusively until they wrapped production.

"Cut!" Matt said. "Sorry, Louie. It's prob'ly the pipes. We'll do it again in a minute. Tara? Fantastic."

"Thank you."

As soon as Uri was finished checking them with his light meter, Tara wriggled out of Louie's embrace and smoothed her clothes and hair as crew members moved around the set, adjusting lights and flags.

"How about a breath mint next time?" she said.

"I ate one already. And what's with the nails? They're digging into my back."

"Just trying to make it real for you, sweetie."

As Tara got distracted by the makeup person, Louie took Matt aside. "We need to talk," he said.

"I'll have a word with her."

"No, forget that. My agent called. They're shooting this indie feature in the UK, and I've been offered a small role playing opposite David Tennant and Emma Watson!"

"Wait," Phoebe said. "I thought you were up for that part in *Roadside Hospital*."

"I didn't get it. I heard it went to Taylor Lautner because he's 'more believable' as a doctor."

"Are you doing a British accent?" Alan said.

Louie looked at him, puzzled. "Oh, I forgot to ask. Anyway, here's the deal. They want me on set in ten days."

Phoebe and Matt exchanged a concerned look. "We'll have to rearrange the schedule," she said. "Let me look at the production board. We might be able to make it work."

"Really? That would be awesome!"

"We'll get back to you," Matt said.

Pumped, Louie walked off, dialing his phone. Alan wandered away with Phoebe. They found Ruby curled up in a corner, asleep. Phoebe took off her jacket and gently covered the girl with it.

"How much longer tonight?" Alan said.

"Well, it looks like we have to do this again. Then, we have another four or five set-ups. We should be here most of the night."

He bent down and tried picking up his daughter without waking her. She groaned in her sleep.

"How many hats do you think Matt owns?"

"I stopped counting after we finished shooting *Yin and Yang*."

"Don't tell me. It's about a guy with a split personality and one of them is a pyscho killer."

She smiled. "Close. They're conjoined twins. One likes to rob banks and the other is a cop. We were sort of going for a Ben Stiller-Jonah Hill vibe."

"Sounds funny." He straightened up. "I'm going to put her to bed. Can we see dailies tomorrow?"

Phoebe's eyes got huge. "Sure."

Matt had moved to the craft services table. He grabbed one of the stale leftover bagels and took a huge bite. When he reached for the coffee, he realized the pot was empty.

"What do I have to do to get some coffee around here?" he said, his voice nasal and petulant.

"I'll see if the kitchen's open," Phoebe said, rolling her eyes.

Alan watched as she ran out, tripping over a huge bundle of black electrical cables and swearing. He walked up to his brother, who was helping himself to another bagel.

"You know," Alan said, "you should treat Phoebe a little nicer."

"Look who's giving me relationship advice."

"I'll see you around."

Everyone was tired, and they were starting to get on each other's nerves. Matt discussed the next shot with Uri as Alan carried Ruby out, being careful to step over the cables.

"Let's do this!" Matt said, grabbing a paper coffee cup from Phoebe, without so much as a thank-you.

As Alan made his way with Ruby down a shadowy hallway toward their rooms, two crew members rushed past, one of whom looked as if he was about to heave.

"Something he ate!" the other one said.

It was quiet again. Alan stopped to adjust his grip on his daughter. When he turned around, he saw Klaus Becker, dressed as the caretaker, standing in front of him and looking like the ghost of Hamlet's father.

"I never had children," the German said. His voice had the air of vague portent that might have been the prelude to a witch's curse.

"Excuse us," Alan said, indicating his sleeping daughter. "We're both dead. *Tired!* Dead tired."

∾

RUBY HERE. Voices in the hallway woke me, and when I opened my eyes I was in my room, lying on my bed. The last thing I remembered was being on set. Had Dad carried me all the way back? Wow, I really do sleep like the dead. I seemed to recall a strange conversation with someone who had a German accent. Oh right, the creepy caretaker.

"Dad?"

"In here," he said.

I yawned and stretched, then wandered into his room. He was sitting at the desk with the lamp on, making notes in his script.

"I'm sorry," he said, "but that guy playing the caretaker is not even close to the character I wrote. I told Matt and Phoebe I had envisioned Morgan Freeman, and instead, they give me Tobin Bell."

"I know what you mean."

"And what about the woman playing his wife? She sounds like she's from Transylvania, for crying out loud."

"You know, Dad, those two would be perfect if this was a horror movie," I said.

"Huh, you're right. Hey, what are you doing up, anyway?"

Message received. "Night, Dad." I yawned loudly and wandered back into my room.

"Good night, baby. Brush your teeth!"

IN THE HALLWAY outside Sam and Kate's room, muffled voices spoke playfully. A thin shadow moved slowly across the wall toward the door, its extremities elongated like slender tree branches. Far off, the hissing noise persisted.

"Shame on me for thinking about professional sports," Sam said from inside.

"Who needs a professional when you can have an amateur?"

"What is that noise?"

The door flew open and Sam stepped out into the hallway, but he didn't find anything. As he turned to go back inside, a hairy hand grabbed his shoulder. His blood turning to ice, he wheeled around and saw one of the guests, a heavyset man in his fifties with a portable oxygen tank and cannula.

"That fire at our hotel was no accident," the man said, struggling to breathe.

"What're you talking about?"

"Listen to me! I used to be a private investigator. Someone set that fire deliberately to get us all to come here. You seem like a bright kid. Meet me tonight in the garden and I'll tell you everything I know."

"Tonight?"

"Sam?" Kate said from inside the room. "What are you doing out there?"

"Be right in!"

"I'm getting in the shower!"

"Please, I gotta go," Sam said to the man.

"Honeymoon, huh?" The man coughed. "Tomorrow morning, then. Early."

He lumbered down the hallway, coughing and breathing heavily, then paused and spoke over his shoulder. "The garden. Near the well."

As Sam watched the man disappear into the shadows, he could hear the sound of the shower running.

Kate stepped out of the shower in a towel and noticed the faint outline of someone in the fogged mirror moving slowly behind her.

"Sam?"

Sam jumped out, a goofy smile on his face, causing Kate to drop her towel.

"Whoops."

"Don't do that," she said, covering herself. "I thought you were a stranger."

"Would a stranger do this?" He kissed her passionately.

Outside, the shadow lingered on the wall by the door, one extremity more pronounced than the others. The beginnings of a crude hand was taking shape.

17

"Oh, no tears please. It's a waste of good suffering."

— HELLRAISER

Nadia sat curled up in a corner of the cozy sitting room, reading *Brecht on Theatre*, her copy of the script lying next to her. The light from the vintage glass table lamp cast a warm, inviting glow. A colorful Afghan lay across her legs. She had never felt so peaceful. Vicky was right.

A noise startled her. Looking up, she saw Becker standing in the shadowy doorway like a lurching demon, his script in his hand. The dimness of the light made his eyes appear icy and hollow. Nadia tensed.

"I thought we could rehearse," he said.

A UCLA linebacker wearing sweats and size sixteen checkerboard Vans rose from an overstuffed chair in the corner. He had been a last-minute addition to the crew and had agreed to protect Nadia in exchange for Outback steaks and Rockstar.

"Can I help you?" His voice was unnaturally high.

"This is Wayne," Nadia said, her tone apologetic.

The bodyguard had been a bad idea; she could see that now. What had she imagined Klaus would do to her? Cut her to pieces with his goring knife?

Becker and Nadia sat uncomfortably on the loveseat with Wayne corkscrewed between them. Each actor held a script and a gel pen. The linebacker, holding a rolled-up *Sports Illustrated*, suppressed a yawn.

"I vowed never to speak of it," Becker said, unable to make eye contact with his acting partner. "I have kept my promise."

"Yes, but now he's escaped," she said, trying to look past the Hulk. "He'll stop at nothing." She broke into uncontrollable laughter. "I'm sorry. This is foolish."

"The script?"

"No. Wayne, it's all right, you don't need to stay."

He hesitated. Grunting, she tried forcing him off the sofa, but it was like trying to move the Carpathians.

"I'll be fine. *Please!*"

He got up to leave, but continued looking back, as if Becker might strangle the old woman with the piano wire the linebacker was sure he kept hidden under his shirt. After Wayne had gone, she smiled guiltily.

"A bodyguard," she said. "What a ridiculous idea."

Becker produced a vicious-looking knife. Nadia shrieked as he calmly examined the blade.

"It's a prop," he said. "See?"

He pressed down on the collapsible blade with his index finger. She tried it herself, giggling with relief, and touched his arm as he put the knife away and went back to his notes.

"You know when you say, 'Yes, but now he's escaped'? It doesn't make sense. We've already established that."

Nodding in agreement, she crossed out the line. Then, she put her script down and put her hand on his.

"Klaus, I was so sorry to hear about your wife."

"You know, the real mystery surrounding Anna's death is, why didn't I love her more? I was never able to solve it."

They sat in silence. Then, Nadia took both his hands in hers. She ran her fingers over the many knife scars.

"I have a confession," she said. "I never had amnesia. I ran away because I was young and foolish. The truth is, I was afraid of our love—afraid it would consume me and I would disappear."

"I was no good for you."

"No, that's not true. I should have stayed with you, Klaus. I loved you so much. I..."

He looked down at her hands holding his and smiled sadly. "I think they should dance."

"What?"

"These two pathetic characters. They have nothing else but each other. They've lost one son, the other is insane. It would be the one thing they have together."

"It's the only way they can express their intimacy," she said, her eyes tearing up.

Excitedly, she took his hand, got to her feet, and pulled him to the middle of the floor. As natural as rain on a rose petal, they danced a waltz to the music in their lonesome souls.

Outside, the first light of day illuminated the sky. Phoebe washed her face as Matt collapsed on the bed with an exaggerated sigh. Annoyed, he reached under his pillow, removed a gory arm, and tossed it on the floor.

"That's it, Uri. I'm getting you tomorrow."

Phoebe came over and sat on the bed, drying her face with a towel and looking at him intently. Uncomfortable, he checked his phone and pretended to yawn.

"What do you see in me?" she said.

"Phoebe, do we have to do this now? I gotta be up in two hours."

"This is exactly what I'm talking about, Matt. You said 'I' when you should have said 'we.' *We* have to be up in two hours." She belted him in the arm.

"Ow! Okay, *we*. Come to bed."

"After I saw your film—"

"*Last Dance.*"

"Yeah. I thought you were this talented, sensitive person. I overlooked the other stuff because, well, because I believed in you. But you've never once treated me like a partner. It's 'Phoebe, do this.' 'Phoebe, do that.' 'How about some more beef jerky, Phoebe?'"

"Yeah, I'm a guy. So what?"

"You're dishonest."

"Dishonest?"

"And you're in denial about it."

"No, I'm not."

"Let's say for a moment you *are* honest with me—which you're not—what about your brother?"

"Alan? Talk about dishonest. Look, Stacey wants to stay home and raise a kid, and he can't deal. I mean, what is the real issue here? I'll tell you. It's his overbearing, ballbuster of a mother."

"We're talking about *you*."

"My mother stayed at home, and look how great I turned out."

If she hadn't been trying to make a point, she would

have laughed in his face. He looked at her with nearly authentic sincerity.

"This is our dream, remember?" he said.

"I don't care. He trusted you with his film, and you're screwing him royally."

"Oh, come on. Are you telling me you believe that fairy tale he wrote in college is gonna save his marriage? Now who's in denial?"

"No, but you made *him* believe it. Face it, Matt. You lied to him so you could make your stupid movie."

"*Our* movie, remember? You lied, too."

"Shit, I know."

She collapsed miserably on the bed and curled up next to him. He fluffed his pillow and lay back down.

"What are we going to do?" she said.

"Let's get some sleep." He reached for her breast. "You thought I was talented?"

"Seriously?" she said, slapping his hand away. "What are we going to do? We have dailies in the morning." Wearily, she shook him with both hands. "Maaaaaatt. Tell me what we're going to do."

He lay there silently, staring at something on the ceiling.

RUBY HERE. It was morning already. I'd slept awesomely and was looking forward to seeing actual footage from our movie. Then, something awful happened. As I fidgeted next to Dad, I tried to think how I could tell him things were, well, not as they seemed. Why did I have to go poking around, anyways? I should've minded my own business.

The sitting room was pretty crazy as everyone, amped on caffeine and sugar, crowded in front of a giant screen set up for a DLP projector. Dad was sipping coffee and chatting with his new BFF Uri. Phoebe and Matt were standing in front of the screen. She did not look well.

"Where's Bailey?" Matt said to Phoebe.

"She's sick."

"Let's get started!" he said. "I want to thank Jade for pulling the footage together so quickly."

A major round of applause erupted for Jade, who was seated up front at her laptop.

"Obviously," Phoebe said, "we have a ways to go, but this will—"

"Enough talking!" someone said.

Everybody else joined in. In spite of the pain in my gut, I found myself hooting and hollering with the rest of the crew. Dad nodded encouragingly to Phoebe and Matt, who looked at each other as if they were about to walk off a cliff. And I knew the reason why.

"Okay, let's go," Matt said, unusually reserved.

One of the grips killed the lights and Jade started the show. At first, it was hard for me to see the same scenes over and over—master shots, close-ups, over-the-shoulders—but soon, I got the hang of it. Sam and Kate driving up the coast. Cute, romantic portraits of the B&B. Sam and Kate enjoying a candlelight dinner. Sam fiddling with the TV remote in their room. Kate in the shower. Of course, Dad tried covering my eyes for that last scene.

When the lights came up, everyone turned to Dad, waiting for his approval. Honestly, it was a little odd.

"Wow," he said. "What can I say? It looks great."

As everyone sighed with relief, Phoebe gave Matt a nervous smile.

"Thanks, Alan," Matt said.

Dad turned to me. "Rube, what did you think?"

I didn't know what to say. Was I supposed to have some sort of outburst in front of everyone? The entire experience had been staged for Dad's benefit, and it was beginning to make me physically ill. But I couldn't speak up, and instead chose to scroll through my old text messages.

Matt clapped his hands. "Thanks, everyone! Uri, I need to see you in my office."

Everyone scattered like chickens as Phoebe and Matt were immediately surrounded by the crew shouting a million questions. I hung back with Dad, waiting for an opening. There wasn't one. The man looked like he was in heaven. His dream—*Endless Honeymoon*—was becoming a reality. Never mind that we hadn't seen a single scene involving conflict. The whole thing looked like one, long travel commercial—something you'd see when you turned on the TV in a hotel room. I couldn't take it anymore.

"Dad, I need to talk to you," I said.

"Can it wait, honey? I promised Matt some new pages."

"But it's important."

"We'll talk at lunch, I promise."

He patted my knee, got up, and walked off. I wandered around in a daze for a while and ended up back in the sitting room, where Matt was going through the shooting script and making notes. I wondered if I should confront him.

"Need something, Ruby?" he said.

"No, just hanging out."

A second later, Louie marched in, super agitated. "We need to talk. My agent called again and—"

The AD rushed in, juggling rolls of toilet paper. "Matt, two more crew members are down."

"Tell Phoebe. I'm busy," Matt said, not looking up.

"I can't find her."

Matt stood. "I don't get it, what's going on?"

"We're pretty sure it's the stomach flu."

Louie pushed the AD aside and stepped directly in front of Matt.

"I'm trying to have a private conversation here? Matt, I need to—"

Uri rushed in, with the best boy on his tail. Then, two more crew members joined them.

"I need Deep Blue gels!" Uri said. "Matt, are you listening? Where are my Deep Blue gels?"

This was the first time I had ever seen Matt flustered. "Phoebe was supposed to—"

"Everybody's throwing up!" the AD said, pushing Louie out of the way and getting up in Matt's grill.

"How am I supposed to shoot the next scene?" Uri said.

Spewing what I could only assume were Russian swear words, Uri shoved the AD out of the way and closed in for the kill. The AD popped up like a cork and got in behind Uri, putting Louie third in line.

"I'm leaving, Matt!" Louie said, trying to get my uncle's attention by waving his arms. "Hello?"

The scene was complete chaos as more crises were introduced, courtesy of unnamed and unsung below-the-line crew members who had signed on to the production because they thought it would be cool working with Matt, but in reality were being treated no better than Roman slaves.

"Will everyone shut up!" Matt said, holding his head to keep it from coming off. "Louie, what're you talking about?"

"I gotta go, or I'll miss my shot!" he said.

Uri snorted. "Deep Blue gels, Matt! I need Deep Blue gels!"

The AD inched closer. "It's a puking pandemic out there!"

Matt ignored the others and concentrated on Louie. "But you still have scenes!"

Louie stamped his foot like a spoiled child. "Emma Watson, man! Are you kidding me?"

"I need you to finish this movie, Louie!"

"Aw, man! How long?"

"I don't know! That's Phoebe's department!"

"End of the week, Matt! After that, I'm gone!"

Louie stomped out, refusing to acknowledge Tara, who was standing at the door. The others saw their chance and closed in like a pack of hungry vampires.

"Phoebe, I need Phoebe!" Matt said, collapsing onto the sofa.

"She's in the bathroom," Tara said, her arms folded across her chest. "Gacking her guts out."

I MANAGED to find Dad and persuaded him to join me in the garden. We walked past a wooden bench in front of an old well that had been boarded up. Grips passed by randomly, hauling lights and stands. Then, the property master appeared, carrying a severed leg under each arm. When he saw us, he darted the other way. Everything made perfect sense. What would Dad do once he knew the truth?

A window on the second floor of the B&B was open, and someone was using a rope to haul up a naked, gored-out woman's body. I cringed every time the realistic-looking head banged into the wall. Fortunately, Dad was facing away from the building and didn't see a thing.

"I wish the movie was finished. The editing, the music."

"Uh-huh," I said, rolling and unrolling the script I was holding.

"I have to confess, I never really saw how a movie could save my marriage, but I want to do this, Ruby. I think your mom would—"

"Dad, they're not making your movie!" I said.

I lowered my voice as more crew members moved past us. A noise made Dad turn around, just as the woman's body disappeared inside the second-story window.

"There are bound to be changes, honey. I expected that."

Though I didn't want to, I opened the script to the title page and handed it to him, closing my eyes in preparation for Armageddon.

"It's a horror movie," I said.

"*Chainsaw Chuck*? But this isn't—" He skimmed the first few pages. "What is this? We didn't shoot this." He turned the page. "'The kid's pale hand, bloody and lifeless...' Ruby, where did you get this?"

I couldn't even look my father in the eye. I wished I was in Amityville. This whole stupid adventure had been my idea. And now, everything was one, big, steaming pile of... We were going to lose Mom for sure.

"I sort of stole it from the script supervisor," I said.

"Bailey?"

"While she was in the bathroom throwing up."

He tore through the screenplay, looking for something familiar. "Here, look. This is our scene." He turned to another page. "Oh, no—"

"Dad, this is the shooting script they're working from. The *real* script. Don't you get it? They're doing a mash-up. They left a few copies of *Endless Honeymoon* lying around just for show."

"Which means they're all in on it," Dad said, his eyes narrowing.

He took a slow, deep breath. I wondered what thoughts of murder and mayhem were going through his mind. I was scared—for Matt.

"Dad?"

"I'll kill him," he said.

He left me standing in the garden, staring at a bloody torso someone had forgotten under the bench.

18

"Who's going to believe a talking head? Get a job in a sideshow."

— Re-Animator

The first thing Jade did after moving in was to convert her room into an edit bay. She had taken down the artwork and lined the walls with dozens of 3x5 cards. A Mac Pro sat on the desk, hooked up to large dual monitors and speakers. Next to it sat a row of high-capacity external hard drives. An empty carafe of green tea stood on a nightstand, along with a pile of used teabags. Empty Styrofoam cups littered the floor.

Ignoring the constant cramping in her stomach, Jade checked her notes one more time, after which she replayed a particular sequence—Sam approaching the heavyset man in the garden. As the scene played on one monitor, a stream of metadata appeared on the other. Onscreen, the man was seated with his oxygen tank at a bench next to the well, which was now open. He didn't acknowledge Sam.

"Hey, so what did you wanna show me?" Sam said.

Sam moved closer. He noticed that the man's eyes were closed and his jacket collar was turned up. Gently, Sam touched his shoulder to wake him. The man's head rolled off, bounced off the bench, and landed in the grass, not quite eyes-up.

Jade paused the scene, made a note, and searched for an alternate take. She was about to insert a close-up of the head landing perfectly when an urgent knock at the door interrupted her. She had posted a sign on the door that read ENTER UNDER PAIN OF DEATH. *Can't people read?* At first, she ignored the persistent knocking, but when it wouldn't stop, she got up to answer the door.

RUBY HERE. It felt to me like Dad had been banging on the door for five minutes. At one point, I thought he was going to kick it in. We heard the door unlock, and the editor Jade was staring at us, her mouth open. I could tell she was nervous. Dad was holding the script I'd given him, and his left eye was twitching pretty bad.

"Is Matt in there?" he said.

"No."

Jade was small—about my size—but she was also strong. She tried closing the door and almost succeeded. But Dad got the upper hand and, forcing the door open, pushed past her.

"Oh!"

She scurried after us as we approached her work area. The place looked amazing. As Dad ignored Jade pulling on his arm, I read some of the cards on the wall. Most contained notes about shots Dad and I had never seen before.

"Hey, you can't be in here!" she said.

Dad removed her hand. "My checkbook says I can."

He nodded to me, and I took a seat at the computer. When the editor tried to stop me, Dad bear-hugged her. Poor girl.

"Sorry about this," he said. "I'm not mad at you, Jade."

"Matt!" Jade said, trying to wriggle out of Dad's powerful embrace.

While this was going on, I played back the current sequence. Dad and I watched the screen, fascinated, as Sam made his grisly discovery in the garden. Uri had photographed it beautifully, especially the part with the head. It looked to me like he'd been influenced by *Sleepy Hollow*.

"What are you doing?" someone said.

I turned to find Matt at the door. Jade back-kicked Dad in the shin and pulled free.

"Ow!"

"I'm sorry, Matt. He forced his way in here," the editor said, smoothing her hair and clothes and giving Dad the stink eye.

Dad pointed at the monitor. "Nice scene, Matt. Scary."

I didn't know what to do, so I got up and moved away from the computer. Pushing aside a pink bra, Dad hopped onto the bed. Then, seeing the severed head on the floor, he picked it up and tossed it from hand to hand like a basketball. He had this crazed Joe Pesci look in his eyes.

Phoebe appeared in the doorway, weak and pale, with what looked like dried vomit on her shirt.

"Shit!" she said.

Dad waved her over. "Come in, Phoebe. Hey, you don't look so good."

She made a face and belched up something from hell.

"Nice," Dad said. "We were about to have a little impromptu production meeting about *Endless Honeymoon.* Oh, that's right, now we're calling it"—Taking his time, he placed the script on his lap, wet his finger, and opened it to the title page—*"Chainsaw Chuck."*

"I'll come back later," Jade said.

Phoebe and Matt watched miserably as she slipped out of the room. Suddenly, the severed head hit Matt hard in the temple, knocking off his cap. He spun wildly like Roger Rabbit and sank to the floor.

"Stop it!" Phoebe said.

"Dad!"

Dad looked over at his brother. "He'll live."

Phoebe was kneeling down and examining the ugly bruise forming on Matt's head. They both stared at Dad, who was flipping through the screenplay without reading it.

"I'm curious about this opening sequence in the asylum," he said. "When exactly were you planning on shooting that?"

"We filmed it last year," Phoebe said, her voice barely above a whisper.

"You mean, when you tried making this movie the first time. When were you going to tell me, Matt? The night of the screening? In front of my wife and daughter?"

Matt tried getting up, but he was still pretty wobbly. He leaned on Phoebe for support until he could regain his balance.

"I was trying to figure out a way to tell you," he said.

"How about 'Alan, you know that movie I was making for you to help you get your wife back? Funny story…'"

"All right."

"'...it's actually a horror movie. But guess what? Those make great date movies, too.'"

"I get it."

"'Ask Rob Zombie.'"

I would have given anything to be back home, listening to Mom banging on her stupid cowbell. Instead, I got to witness Dad leaping off the bed and attacking his only brother. Two grown men in a very small hotel room—not ideal. Phoebe and I stared at each other as Matt rolled, scrambled to his feet, grabbed the fake head, and tried beating my father senseless with it as Dad reached out with both hands to choke the life out of his assailant.

Phoebe tried taking away the prop. "Stop it! We still need that!"

"Are you both crazy?" I said.

I came around and joined Phoebe. Instinctively, we held hands. Dad and Matt were on their feet now. Matt was about to take a swing when he stopped, turned around, and darted out the door like a scared bunny.

Dad went after him. "You can run, but you can't hide, Matt!"

"I don't believe this!" Phoebe said.

I nodded. "We'd better follow them."

As we came out into the hallway, I saw Dad disappearing around a corner, yelling obscenities. I ran ahead, but Phoebe was still weak and had to walk. Rounding the corner, I saw Matt leaping over cables and dodging light stands like a traceur. Dad tried doing the same but ended up knocking everything down. Then, he tripped over a junction box and landed face-first on the floor.

"Are you okay?" I said, helping him up.

"I'm still going to kill him."

Muttering something, Dad took off again as Matt ran out the French doors into the garden. Phoebe had caught up, and together, we continued outside. It was pretty obvious neither of these guys knew how to fight, because they kept throwing these wild punches. A crowd consisting of guests and crew had gathered, and we watched as the two brothers went at it. Finally, they managed to connect, hitting each other in the face at the same time. Both stumbled backward and landed on the grass opposite each other, breathing like woolly mammoths.

Dad, sporting a fresh black eye, was the first to get up. Wiping blood from his swollen lip, Matt looked at him warily. But instead of kicking the life out of his brother, Dad hung back.

"I trusted you with my heart, Matt," he said and staggered away. "I'm shutting down the production."

As I stood there, helpless, Phoebe went to Matt and knelt next to him.

"You can't do that!"

"Shut up, Matt," she said as she probed his lip.

"Ow! Cut it out!"

DAD and I didn't speak the whole way back. After a couple of lame attempts at pointing out the high quality of the production, I gave up and spent the rest of the trip with my earbuds in, listening to my "Hell and Damnation" playlist—you don't even want to know—and Snapchatting with Claire and Diego. It was the worst road trip I had ever been on.

When we got back to the apartment, I carried my stuff to my room and shut the door. I could hear Dad's answering machine blaring in his home office. Who even owns an answering machine anymore?

"Alan, it's Phil," a voice said. "Listen, I took a look at the papers from Van Loon's attorney. We need to—" *Click.*

I was worried about Dad. I'd never seen him lose his shit like that before. It was pretty darn scary, let me tell you. I thought I'd better check on him and found him standing in front of his computer. The screensaver displayed a photo montage from my parents' wedding. Cursing, he swept everything off the desk and threw his video cartridges into the trash. Taking a deep breath, he hit the home phone's speaker button and made a call.

"Hey, Gina, it's Alan. Is he in?"

She lowered her voice. "He doesn't want to talk to you."

"Please, Gina. Can you ask him?"

I could hear Rick's tinny voice swearing at Gina in the background. Then, he came on the line.

"Yeah?" he said.

"Rick?" Dad tried his best to sound upbeat. "So, I got the papers. Listen, I want to make things right."

"Talk to my attorney."

"Rick, wait. Can't we, uh, can't we work out some kind of settlement?"

There was a long pause. "What did you have in mind?"

"How about I pay your medical bills and give you something for pain and suffering? Rick, we don't need lawyers."

"I'll have to think it over."

Dad's body seemed to relax. "There's something else. I want my job back." Rick cackled like a hyena. "I'm serious. I need to work."

"You should've thought of that before you boiled my nuts."

"I'm a good salesman—the best. Come on, I'll bet your numbers are way down since I left."

"As a matter of fact, we're doing great."

"They're down, Alan," Gina said in the background.

"Gina, what the—"

"So you'll think about it?" Dad said.

Another long pause. Then, "I'll think about it."

Dad disconnected, rubbed the back of his neck, and turned around to find me leaning against the doorframe.

"I guess you heard all that."

"You're not going back to work for that guy? He's an asshat."

"Hey, watch your language!"

"It's true, and you know it."

"What am I supposed to do?"

"Dad, you're a top salesman. Find another dealership." He shook his head. "How's your eye?"

"Hurts a little."

"You should put a steak on it."

"You don't fool me, kiddo. You're just trying to score a steak dinner."

"Guilty as charged. So, can we go?"

"Why not?"

"Really? Where?"

"Pacific Dining Car?"

"Oh my gosh, yes!" I said. "But first, I need to take a shower." I stopped in mid-stride. "Are you sure they're going to let you in there with that eye?"

"Shut up and shower."

I could tell Dad was feeling better.

19

"I'm coming apart! Oh, mother of God, I'm coming apart!"

— THE AMITYVILLE HORROR (1979)

Stacey carefully placed a recent marketing award in a record storage box, along with her other things. She had already decided to leave her business cards behind. On her desk stood a picture of Ruby taken at her eleventh birthday party. She stopped and thought about that day.

As friends and family gathered in the dining room, Ruby blew out the candles on her cake. Everyone—including her friends Claire and Diego—cheered. Setting down a stack of cake plates, Stacey touched Alan's shoulder. He lowered the video camera.

"She's growing up, and I've missed so much of it," she said.

"Come on, look how happy she is."

"You don't understand."

Ruby had ripped open a huge present and found a new

computer inside. Lots of oohs and ahhs. She smiled as Diego took pictures.

Stacey lay the precious photo on top of her other things and headed out of her office for the last time. Separating from Alan had been difficult, but her intuition told her things were about to get even more bizarre.

WARREN MUDGE, wearing a blue cast on his left arm, stood at the window of his office, using his binoculars to watch the lonely *paletero* selling ices below on the steps of the building. Behind him on the desk sat the rosewood ring box. The doctors had been shocked at Warren's rapid recovery, and he was experiencing only moderate pain now. Since the accident, he had come to believe he was superhuman, a notion that had been floating around in his head since his college pole-vaulting days. Superhuman people were not only strong, he reasoned, but they could also fly.

Slipping the ring box into his jacket pocket, Warren left his office without telling anyone and rode the elevator to the top floor. From there, he climbed the emergency stairs to the roof. It was windier than he had expected. A helicopter was about to lift off from the roof of a nearby building. He smiled and, on an impulse, waved to the two executives in suits boarding the craft.

Breathing deeply and doing a few stretches, he strode to the edge and climbed up over the safety railing, confident his plan would succeed. Using his binoculars, he checked to see if the *paletero* was still down there. He also made sure he had cash on him. Today, he would try the *aguacate*. Setting the binoculars on the ledge, Warren looked up to see the helicopter circling nearby. He wished he weren't wearing a cast. Then again, superhumans didn't care about things like that.

It took him only a few seconds to make it all the way down. No one noticed the body hitting the ground, because it had landed behind a row of dogwood shrubs. Besides, everyone was busy buying their favorites off the *paletero's* cart.

RUBY HERE. The next afternoon I found Dad in the living room, staring at the photograph of Mom, him, and me. He wiped his eyes. I was going to say something supportive, but I realized he would get all "Dad" on me and pretend it was only his allergies acting up.

"Hey," I said.

When he saw me, he reached out and pulled me close. I felt another bear hug coming on, but decided to let him express himself the only way he knew. He held me close and stroked my hair—something he hadn't done since I was little. It was strangely comforting.

"This is my fault," he said.

"Daddy, that's not true." *Wait, had I just called him 'Daddy'?* "Matt tricked you."

"No, honey, I mean everything. We would have never come to this place if...if only I'd listened to your mother."

"Well, maybe she won't go through with it," I said. But he wasn't buying it. "Everything will be fine."

"*I'm* supposed to say that."

I didn't have any idea how long we remained that way, but the whole time I was thinking I had to do something. But what? *Think, Ruby!* Nothing. I needed my friends around me now.

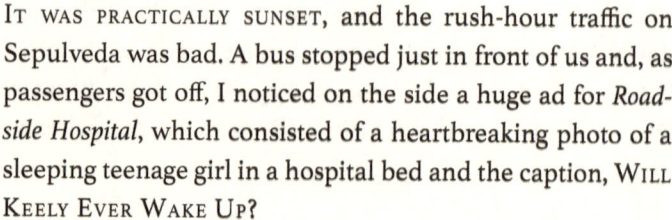

I<small>T WAS PRACTICALLY SUNSET</small>, and the rush-hour traffic on Sepulveda was bad. A bus stopped just in front of us and, as passengers got off, I noticed on the side a huge ad for *Roadside Hospital*, which consisted of a heartbreaking photo of a sleeping teenage girl in a hospital bed and the caption, W<small>ILL</small> K<small>EELY</small> E<small>VER</small> W<small>AKE</small> U<small>P</small>?

Claire, Diego, and I were sitting at one of the outdoor tables at Tito's Tacos, another favorite hangout. On school holidays, we would head over around lunchtime to see if we could spot any industry people from nearby Sony Pictures. Usually the only ones we encountered were sweaty IT guys wearing jeans, faded polo shirts, and trade show backpacks, hoping to meet girls.

I sat there picking at my beef burrito as Diego explained the facts of life. Again. Since Claire was the only one with a normal family, she only half-listened as she scrolled through Instagram pics on her phone.

"I don't see how you can stop what's happening," Diego said. "You're a kid."

"I have to try." That came out angrier than I had intended.

"Sometimes things are meant to be, Ruby."

"Like cramps," Claire said.

"No, Diego, I can't accept that. This is America. We have choices."

Somewhere mixed in with the traffic noises, I could hear a bell tinkling. I looked over and noticed a *paletero*, with one leg shorter than the other, coming toward us. I'd seen him around LA from time to time and always wondered who he was. Now, Claire and Diego were looking at him. As he passed us, he smiled at Diego and continued down the sidewalk.

Diego got up. "BRB."

"Okay..." Claire said.

Confused, we watched Diego follow the *paletero* to the corner. They looked like they knew each other, and I could hear them speaking Spanish. The *paletero* opened his cart and handed Diego three *paletas*—on the house, apparently. Diego kissed him on the cheek and came back over, smiling. He handed us each a watermelon *paleta* and took his seat, as if nothing had happened.

"Okay, so you're not going to explain?" I said.

Diego unwrapped his *paleta* and took a bite. "He's my dad."

"What? Why didn't you tell us before?"

"I didn't think it was important."

"We're your friends, Diego," Claire said. "We have a right to know these things."

The wheels in my head were turning. "So does he speak English?"

"Sure."

Smiling, I got up. "BRB."

"Huh?" Claire said.

I had no idea what I was doing. I ran after the *paletero* as he crossed the street.

"Wait!"

We walked the rest of the way together, saying nothing. When we got to the other side, he stopped and smiled at me. I had never actually seen him up close. He was older than Dad, but with Latinos, it was always hard to tell. He didn't look *old*, per se. But he was a little stooped over. It might have had something to do with his legs. I can't explain, but I felt peaceful around him.

"*Muy bonita,*" he said, looking at me in a fatherly way. "*¿Eres la novia?*"

Though I had taken Spanish, I wasn't very conversational.

"I'm sorry, but I don't speak Spanish."

Novia...novia... Wait, did he think I was Diego's girlfriend?

"No, see, um. *Soy la amiga.* Friend. I wanted to ask you a question about Diego's mom. Did you ever try and, you know, get her back?"

"Why?"

"I don't know. Because you love her?"

"Yes, I love her. *Con todo mi corazón.*"

With all my heart? None of this made any sense. And why was I crying?

"Then, why didn't you try?"

He looked at me with his kind eyes, and I knew he understood what it was I was asking, even though I wasn't sure myself. He touched my shoulder and shook his head sadly, saying something to himself in Spanish that I couldn't hear.

"*I* left *her, mija,*" he said.

"What? But I thought—"

"She deserves a prince. One day..."

I felt dizzy, like the world was spinning off its axis. As the *paletero* wandered away, a young Latina ran up to him and bought a *paleta,* smiling at him through missing front teeth. Then, a strange thing happened. I saw Dad bending down, giving the girl her treat. I rubbed my eyes, and when I looked again, the vendor had disappeared into a crowd of pedestrians, his little bell still tinkling.

I wandered back, feeling more confused than ever, and oblivious to everything around me. Vaguely, I heard horns honking as I drifted across the street, returned to our table, and plopped myself down.

"Ruby, what were you guys talking about?" Claire said.

"What? Oh, I was asking Diego's dad where he got the *paletas*. They're delicious." Then to Diego, "Do you get to see him much?"

"Pretty regular. He promised to take me to Puerto Vallarta once he's saved enough money."

"I'm sorry, Diego. It must be so hard to—"

"It's all good."

Claire and I exchanged a look. We both knew that's what people say when there's no hope.

I HAD TO DO SOMETHING. No way was I going to end up the estranged daughter of a car salesman. It was only a rough plan, but I figured I could pull it off. After dinner, Dad was sitting in the living room, drinking coffee, and half-reading the *Los Angeles Times* "Calendar" section. On TV, some talking head on ESPN was blathering about the LA Rams' upcoming season. Clearing my throat, I went into my act.

"Dad? This whole thing with Matt has me very upset."

He was ignoring me. "Uh-huh."

"I need Mom."

"Then, give her a call."

"No, I'm too upset! Haven't you been listening?"

"I'll call her in the morning."

"Now!" I said, sending my voice into the dolphin range.

As I blubbered pathetically into my hands, Dad handed me the "Sports" section—presumably for me to wipe my nose—and grabbed his phone, which he almost dropped taking it out of his pocket. It's a well-known fact men are physically incapable of dealing with weeping women.

"Hey, Stace," he said, his eyes shifting between me and the floor. "No, everything's fine, except... What? Um, she's here...crying."

On cue, I let out a pathetic wail as Dad handed me the phone.

"Mommy?"

20

"You know, I'll bet my badge right now, we haven't seen the last of those weirdies."

— Plan 9 from Outer Space

I t had taken every bit of my concentration, plus a major dose of luck, to arrange everything. I had even said a prayer that nothing would go wrong. Now, standing in the kitchen of my mother's house, I calmed myself using a breathing technique I'd picked up in a parks and rec yoga class. Mom was busy making us root beer floats —her sure-fire cure for what ails ya. At least I was getting ice cream out of the deal.

"Thanks," I said as she handed me mine. "I miss these."

"Mm-hm."

"Where's Ed?"

"Oh, he's around."

I didn't know if it was my imagination, but Mom seemed a little suspicious. It must've been me. How could she suspect anything?

"So, what's this big crisis?" she said. "Was going on vacation with your father that terrible?"

"No, it was great. I wanted to..."

I hated stalling. But timing was everything. As I was about to suggest a board game, the doorbell rang, and I ran to answer it.

"I'll get it!"

"Ruby, what—"

I flung the front door open and found Phoebe smiling. She had dressed for the occasion, wearing a black leather jacket, white cashmere sweater, flouncy black skirt, and black Doc Martens I now craved.

"Come in!" I said, using my stage voice. "What a surprise."

As I helped my friend with her backpack, Mom came over, her arms folded in an attitude of pure judgment. Though she possessed a sonar system the Navy would die for, I carried on as if the whole affair were innocent.

"Oh, Mom. This is Phoebe Conklin. Matt's girlfriend?"

"Hi, Mrs. Navarro."

"Call me Stacey. Girls, what's this about?"

"What do you mean?" I said.

"Ruby, I'm not your father. Give me some credit."

I glanced at Phoebe, whose cheeks had flushed.

"Fine, I'll fess up," I said. "But first we're going to need another root beer float."

THE THREE OF us sat in the kitchen eating our ice cream. Ed had joined us and had parked himself next to Phoebe. Mom waited patiently, her shrewd eyes moving from one of us to the other like a Felix the Cat wall clock. Neither Phoebe nor I wanted to go first.

"Boy, this is great," Phoebe said.

I nudged her. "Right?"

"Enough with the Yelp reviews," Mom said. "Which one of you is going to tell me what's going on?"

Phoebe and I exchanged a nervous look. I cleared my throat unnecessarily as Phoebe took my hand under the table.

"Mom, Dad's in, like, serious trouble."

"Mm-hm. Go on."

"It sort of has everything to do with you."

She pursed her lips and looked at Phoebe. "And this concerns you how?"

I got up, leaned over the table, and grabbed Mom's wrist, forcing her to look at me. It was a bold move, but I knew what I was doing.

"Before she answers, I need to know," I said. "Are you and Warren Mudge getting married?"

For a second, Mom was speechless—something I thought I'd never witness. She leaned back and covered part of her face with her hand.

"Ruby, this is a personal matter. I don't think—"

"Mom, *please!* We don't have much time!"

She looked at both of us, sighed, and turned away, covering her left hand with her right.

"No," she said. "I'm not marrying him. He's, um... You see, he passed away."

I jumped up, knocking over my chair, and did a happy dance.

"Thank God! Not about him being dead, but... So, that means you and Dad can get back together and—"

"Ruby," Phoebe said.

"I hate that stupid apartment. This is going to be great. We should go to Disneyland!"

"Hey, hey, hold on!" Mom said. "First, show a little respect. This is no time to celebrate—a man died. And second, this doesn't change anything between your father and me. Sit down."

"But..." I sank into a chair.

"Look. Everything Warren promised me was— It validated what I want to do. But that's no reason to marry someone. I'd made my decision *before* the, um, the accident. And as for your father... Sure, I could go back with him, but eventually, we'd have the same problems."

"But if you really love him—" I said, getting upset all over again.

"Sweetie, this isn't some fairy tale. It's real life. And in real life, there aren't always happy endings. It's time you learned that."

The three of us sat there without speaking. Phoebe played with her spoon while I tried sculpting what was left of my ice cream into a spike so I could impale my head on it.

"Now can you two *please* explain what's going on?" Mom said.

Before I could answer, Phoebe said, "Mrs. Navarro, your husband has been trying to find a way to secretly get you back into your marriage. That isn't over yet."

"What? Did Alan put you up to this?"

"No-uh!" I said.

Phoebe continued. "He thought if he could make this movie, you would—"

"Wait a second, did you say 'movie'?"

Phoebe was in the zone, and I sat back and watched as she went into pitch mode.

"Well, he wrote this screenplay in college, right? And he

thought if he made it into a movie, you'd see how good your relationship was—*is*. And you'd want to get back together. I think it's very cool."

She leaned back and took a huge bite of ice cream. I gave her a thumbs-up on the sly.

"This makes no sense," Mom said, getting to her feet and clearing the table.

I handed her my goblet. "Look, it's very simple. Dad started off with our home movies, right? But they sucked, and then, he got fired—"

"Your father got fired?"

"Yes, for pouring boiling coffee down Rick Van Loon's pants."

"But why would he do that?"

"Because he was defending your honor, Mom! Try and keep up."

"Then, he got caught up in this movie," Phoebe said. "He put up the financing and everything."

Mom set the dishes on the counter and collapsed onto one of the bar stools. It was as if she was having a conversation with herself, replaying everything in her head.

"I always knew Alan was a little wrong in the head. After we were married, he insisted on investing thirty thousand dollars in a thoroughbred who he said was going to win the Triple Crown. Turned out the horse was flat-footed and had a morbid fear of starting gates. And other horses. But a *movie?*"

She held up her hand to stop us from going on. Then, she wandered around in the kitchen, straightening things that were already straight. From the look on her face, I could tell she was trying to put the pieces together. Without warning, she broke into uncontrollable giggling. I was worried she'd lost it.

"Mom?" I said.

She planted herself in front of us. "Are you saying he was actually trying to make *Endless Honeymoon*?"

"You know about that?"

"Oh, boy! I read that thing years ago. It's terrible."

"That's what I was saying!" Phoebe said.

The three of us sat on bar stools at the counter, gorging on Ben & Jerry's Half Baked and assorted cookies and snack cakes. I hadn't gotten this kind of a sugar high since a sleepover in sixth grade when Piper Di Francesco talked us into bedazzling her aged Dachshund-Corgi mix.

"And Matt thought he could make this bloody horror movie using the same actors without Alan ever finding out," Phoebe said, spraying cookie crumbs everywhere as she laughed uncontrollably.

I winked at Mom. "Like Dad would be that lame. He would've figured it out eventually."

"Hmm," Mom said.

"Mom!"

"Ruby, I'm sorry, but your father is very gullible. Though it is one of the things that attracted me to him."

"So, now you love him again?"

She sighed. "Ruby, you see with men... How can I put this? It's like the five stages of dying. Denial, anger, bargaining, depression, and acceptance. Even though we're not together anymore, I've come to accept your father as he is."

"I think I'm still at depression," Phoebe said, using her pinky to dig the filling out of a Malomar.

Mom folded her hands together over one knee. "Okay, bring me up to speed. Where are we?"

"After he found out the truth, Alan fought with Matt and shut down the production," Phoebe said. "Half the crew is sick. We've got enough money to last until the end of the week. Oh, and we're about to lose one of our lead actors."

"Louie?" I said.

"Yeah, he—"

"You mean, they're still on location?" Mom said.

Phoebe shook her head sadly. "Matt couldn't bring himself to tell them yet. He's hanging on by a thread."

Mom got quiet for a moment as we nibbled at our desserts. I had moved on and was already imagining how I would redecorate my second bedroom at Dad's apartment. Maybe some new curtains. And a Lava Lamp.

"What's this thing called?" Mom said.

Phoebe glanced at me, looking confused. *"Chainsaw Chuck?"*

"I like it. Can I see whatcha got so far?"

I had a serious headache and was having a hard time concentrating. From the look on Phoebe's face, she wasn't doing much better.

"Mom, are you serious?"

"Why not? You know how much I love horror movies. It's your father who's into those sappy love stories. *Titanic.* Puh-leeze!"

IN THE HOME OFFICE, Mom and I stood anxiously behind Phoebe as she connected her laptop to the big monitor and opened a browser window.

"Give me a sec," she said. "I had Jade upload a low-res proxy to the school's extranet. The quality won't be the best, but you'll get the general idea."

In a few seconds, she found what she was looking for—a list of files with cryptic names. She clicked on a hyperlink, put the video in full-screen mode, and cranked up the volume on the speakers. For the next hour, we watched the work-in-progress. Jade had done so much more, stringing together scenes—including the insane asylum footage— that seemed to flow beautifully. The story was actually starting to come together—a young couple trying to enjoy their romantic honeymoon while a crazed killer terrorized the inn, leaving bodies everywhere.

When it was over, Phoebe and I looked at Mom, unsure what to expect. She could barely contain her excitement.

"Can we see it again?" she said.

IT WAS LATE, and we had moved the show to the living room. Phoebe and I lay on the floor, down from our sugar highs, as Mom paced excitedly. I never realized old people had so much energy.

"I see what you're trying to do with this movie," she said.

Phoebe tried and failed to sit up because Ed was currently taking a nap on her stomach.

"We never would have gotten this far without Alan's script," she said. "All Matt and I had was the gory stuff. We needed a love story."

I didn't even attempt to sit up, but instead, rolled over onto my side. "Yeah, I can't believe how good it looks so far."

"You know, girls," Mom said, "I think there's an audience for this movie. It's all in how you market it. I mean, you've got romance, you've got scary. There's humor... I'm in."

That got us both up.

"Mom, what do you mean?"

"I want to help. I want us to finish this movie. How about we go up there tomorrow?"

"But we're out of money," Phoebe said.

"Leave that to me."

I got to my feet, not at all sure what I was hearing. "Mom, what're you saying?"

"I'm saying that I am Phoebe and Matt's new best friend."

Phoebe scrambled to her feet, and we high-fived each other.

MIDNIGHT CAME AND WENT. Phoebe crashed in the guest bedroom after telling Matt the good news. Unable to sleep, I lay in bed, reading the "official" *Chainsaw Chuck* shooting script. A copy of *Endless Honeymoon* lay next to Ed. Though Matt had made a good start, it would take a miracle to turn these two stories into a movie people would love.

Mom knocked softly and came in. "Looks like you can't sleep either," she said.

I handed her both scripts. "You should probably read these."

"Thanks, I will. How is Matt shooting this from two screenplays?"

"Phoebe told me he's relying a lot on Jade. The magic of editing, I guess. Mom, do you really think we'll be able to pull it off?"

"Hey, we're three smart cookies. We'll figure it out."

"There's something I don't understand. How can you just take off work like this?"

"Yeah... I quit my job."

"What? Because your boss died?"

She sat on the bed, touched my face, and tucked my hair

back behind my ear—something she hadn't done in a long time.

"Let's just say it's not a very comfortable place to work right now," she said. "People knew what was going on between Warren and me. I mean, it wasn't much of a secret. After I made my decision not to marry him, I was worried my co-workers would treat me differently."

"Oh."

"It's funny. I always thought I'd leave because I had married Warren to stay at home. I never considered what would happen if I *didn't* marry him. Then he died, of course."

"Are you sad?"

"About him? Yes. He was a great boss. I'm also sad about my job. I loved working there. But hey, I'm excited, too. About this movie."

"Mom, not to pry but, like, what'll you do about money?"

"Don't worry. I've made some good investments, so I should be okay for a while. We'll finish *Chainsaw Chuck*—or whatever we're calling it—then I'll start looking for another job. The market's pretty good right now."

She kissed me again and stood. If you'd asked me, that plan had Chernobyl written all over it, but I decided to be supportive.

"Sounds great, Mom," I said.

"Get some sleep, Rubykins. We have a movie to finish."

"Mom? Whatever you decide. You know, about your job, the baby... I promise I'll support your decision."

She hugged me tightly. "Thank you, Ruby. That means everything to me."

"Only you have to promise you won't call me 'Rubykins.'"

"Deal."

Though it was hard for me to believe, I felt like the project was getting back on track. Mom to the rescue! But there was still one very big unknown—something that would determine whether we were saving our family or just wasting time and money on a giant boondoggle.

"About Dad," I said. "When exactly were you planning to tell him?"

21

"All right, dammit. Now we've got a war."

— DAWN OF THE DEAD (1978)

We arrived at Dad's apartment at seven-thirty in the morning. Phoebe had followed Mom and me in her car. Bleary-eyed from no sleep and in need of a shave—and not even curious why we'd brought the dog along—Dad escorted us into the living room, where I noticed the Blu-ray disc of *Titanic* sitting on top of the player, next to a half-empty tissue box. Mom arched her eyebrows and tried to keep from laughing.

It took us only a few minutes to explain the situation. When we were done, Dad stared at us in slack-jawed amazement.

"Are you out of your minds?" he said.

I pretty much expected that reaction. Though I could tell Mom was getting riled, she kept herself in check.

"I don't get it, Alan," she said. "You wanted to make this movie."

"No, I wanted to make *my* movie, *Endless Honeymoon*."

Then, Mom let her sarcasm slip out. "Oh, I remember. The love story of the century."

Dad ignored her. "And now the whole thing is ruined. That's what I get for trusting my lying sleaze of a brother."

He glared at Phoebe, who looked away guiltily. I felt bad for her.

Smiling, Mom turned to the two of us. "Could you girls make us some coffee?" she said.

Relieved, Phoebe and I hurried into the kitchen as Mom cleared her throat, ready to take on Dad. Though we weren't in the room, we could see and hear everything.

"Alan, I understand what you were trying to do. And I appreciate it, believe me. But what made you think I would ever fall for something like *When Sally Met Leopold*? And again, I appreciate the thought."

Dad looked like his head would explode. I tried to remember whether he kept any guns in the apartment.

"Oh, come on!" he said. "For your information, I was trying to make a *home movie*, but Matt and Phoebe—and *your daughter*—talked me into this big production!"

"Oh!" Phoebe and I said.

"Didn't I tell you he was gullible?" Mom said to us, smirking.

"Wait a second. Who are you calling 'gullible'? Sounds like they've got *you* believing you should get aboard this train wreck."

I sensed another barroom brawl coming on, but Mom did something unexpected. She walked up to Dad and gently took his hand. His whole attitude changed. Yep, girl magic in action, folks.

"Does your eye hurt?" she said, trying to touch it.

Sulking, he brushed her hand away. "It's fine."

"Alan," she said. "I read both screenplays last night, and I think they're really good. *Together.* I want to help these kids finish the movie."

On cue, Phoebe and I brought out the coffee.

"Which movie?" Dad said.

Mom smiled. "I woke up this morning at four, and in a flash of brilliance, it came to me. Are you ready? I want us to make *Chainsaw Honeymoon*."

I almost fell over. That *was* brilliant! Why hadn't *I* thought of it? Phoebe and I hugged each other like fast friends at summer camp while Dad nodded and took a sip of coffee.

"It sounds like fun," he said. "But that's not the movie I was trying to make."

My jaw dropped. "Dad, are you kidding me right now? We're moving in a different direction."

"I want to make this movie, Alan," Mom said.

He shrugged. "Who's stopping you?"

He stepped away from her and, using a tissue, carefully wiped the fingerprints off the TV remote. She came up behind him and, using two fingers, walked across his shoulders—one step for each word.

"I was sort of hoping...you'd help, too."

"No, no way."

"Come on, Dad," I said. "It'd be like a family adventure."

I gave him the puppy dog pout. When Phoebe saw me, she made the same face. Then, Mom joined in. It's amazing how good women are at that stupid expression. It didn't work, though. Dad stood there, looking like a butthurt middle schooler. Honestly, *men!*

"Why don't you ask Warren?" he said.

"He's dead!" Phoebe and I said at the same time.

He turned to Mom. "What? You're not—"

"I'll fill you in later," she said, and gave Phoebe and me the stink eye. "I have to help Ruby pack. You can choose to not go, but you're looking after Ed while we're on location."

Mom took my hand and led me off to my bedroom, leaving Dad alone with Phoebe. Nope, nothing awkward about that.

≈

MINUTES HAD PASSED since Stacey and Ruby left the room. Phoebe finished her coffee, rinsed her cup in the sink, and returned to the living room, where she found Alan sifting through his jazz collection.

"I guess I should wait in the car," she said, crouching and giving Ed a belly scratch.

He straightened up and looked at her appraisingly. She was a very nice girl—too good for Matt. When they made eye contact, she stood and cleared her throat, unsure of what to expect.

"Listen, Phoebe," he said. "I don't really blame you for any of this. Matt is a manipulating little piece of—"

"No, it was as much my fault. Alan, you have to believe me, I never wanted it to be this way. We were just trying to make a movie. I'm so sorry I lied to you."

A single tear fell on her cheek. He grabbed the box of tissues and handed it to her.

"Thanks."

"Don't mention it."

He was one of the few men who was taller than her, and she naturally gravitated to his shoulder, where she cried herself out. Not knowing what else to do, he patted her back, straightened her shoulders for her, and gently touched each of her eyes with a tissue, which made her smile.

"So, Matt's up there shooting?"

"Until the money runs out."

"Boy, that guy doesn't give up."

"It's one of the reasons I lo—I respect him."

"Right."

RUBY HERE. Outside on the street, Dad helped me load my stuff into the trunk of Mom's car. Phoebe had already taken off, and Mom was inside the car waiting. I hugged Dad and gave him a kiss, still unable to get my head around the fact that he wasn't coming with us.

"Bye, Dad. We'll call you when we get there."

I hopped into the front seat as Mom started the engine. Dad waved to us, then got a funny look when he noticed the damage on Mom's roof from where Warren had landed. Yeah, Mom had told me the whole sordid story on the way over. Not to speak ill of the dead, but what a screwball!

Dad leaned into the passenger window and spoke to Mom. "What happened to your car?"

"Skydiving accident," she said.

Mrs. Tessenbaum, who had been out walking her dog—the one from my nightmare—approached Dad.

"Hi, Mrs. T," Dad said.

"Such a nice family," I heard her say as we drove away. "You're a lucky boy!"

WEARING his avocado green silk shirt, Alan fidgeted in the black leather-and-steel chair as he waited for the sales manager. He touched his black eye self-consciously, wondering if anyone would notice the makeup. Though Rick had told him he might consider taking him back, Alan thought it would be better to make a fresh start. He hadn't seen the new Mercedes dealership since they moved. It was impressive, with its huge two-story white building and service center discretely located a hundred yards away.

As he sipped his espresso, he wondered what it would be like selling Mercedes vehicles. He had always admired the brand, but he felt the seats were a little uncomfortable. The stiff, unforgiving leather was made for German behinds, not American. Still, their customers were loyal, and he knew he would have no problem making a good living.

"Alan?" someone behind him said.

He rose and, setting down his coffee, turned to find a man who looked ten years younger than him, wearing a black Prada suit, pink silk shirt with matching pocket square, and Italian loafers. He had curly black hair and brown eyes, and looked Middle Eastern. And he wore a lot of gold, Alan noticed.

"Sorry to keep you waiting. I'm Omar."

Alan shook his hand. "Great to meet you. Thanks for seeing me on such short notice. I was just admiring the new roadster out there. All I can say is, wow!"

Omar came around his desk, pulled out two bottles of Voss Artesian water from a small refrigerator, and offered one to Alan.

"Thanks," Alan said. "I'm good."

Omar poured himself a glass of water, took a sip, leaned back with his hands laced behind his head, and looked Alan over. Then, he broke into a huge, toothy smile.

"What?" Alan said.

"Sorry. I can't believe I'm sitting across from the guy who put his sales manager in the hospital."

Alan got a sharp pain in his stomach. "Oh, you heard about that."

"*Everyone* heard about it, though I'd love for you to tell me all the juicy details."

"Look. There was an argument, and I spilled hot coffee on the guy," Alan said. "That's it."

"Down his pants! Dude, you were the talk of the Vampire Lounge. The sales managers from all the luxury dealerships like to meet there once a week. We laughed over that for hours."

Though Alan hadn't noticed, he was sinking deeper and deeper into his chair, almost as if he were melting.

"Was Rick Van Loon there?"

"Hardly," Omar said. "That guy's a tool. As far as we're concerned, he got what he deserved. You know, he called me up one time to see if he could join us. I told him we were meeting at Maple Drive Restaurant."

"But that place has been closed for years."

"Exactly," Omar said, sniggering. "I think he got the message."

"So, I heard you had an opening. I thought you might consider hiring me. I've been a top performer for—"

"Yeah... The thing is, Alan—and I say this with all due respect—you've got anger issues. And we have a reputation to uphold."

The reality of those words hit Alan like a blow to the solar plexus. He noticed Omar had whitened his teeth, and he suddenly had the urge to knock one of them out and leave it on the desk, next to the picture of him with some girl who looked like a *Sports Illustrated* swimsuit model.

"I see," Alan said, getting to his feet. "I appreciate the time."

"No problem."

"You don't think the other sales managers—"

"If it was me, I wouldn't waste my time. Have you tried Kia? Maybe they're hiring."

"Thanks. I'll check it out."

He shook hands and left, unaware he was still holding the empty china demitasse. On the way out, he set it on the assistant's desk. *Time to suck up*, he thought, a bitter taste already coating his gums.

Rick Van Loon sat at his desk, smiling at Alan, who was sitting across from him. Rick was no longer wearing the cervical collar and, for the first time in his life, he felt superior.

Alan got to his feet. "I need a cup of coffee."

"*I'll* get it," Rick said.

As Rick crossed over to the credenza, Alan could hear a distinct click-squeak. He scanned the floor, trying to see if there was a mouse in the room.

"Thanks," he said as Rick handed him a cup. "What was that noise?"

Grimly, Rick pointed to his groin. "Ice."

"I'm really sorry about that."

"They admitted me to the burn ward, you know. A nurse had to slather me up with antibiotic cream twice a day."

"That sounds like fun."

"His name was Pablo."

"Oh," Alan said. "Listen, Rick, before we talk about the lawsuit and my possibly working here again, can I ask you a question?"

Rick adjusted his ice pack as he sat down. "Sure, one question."

"What is this thing you have about Stacey?"

"Oh, you wanna talk about Stacey now? Great. Here's the thing. *I* should've been the one to sell her that car, not you."

And there it was. At last. For years, Alan had suspected Rick secretly lusted after his wife, but he could never prove anything. It was the little off-handed remarks. *How's Stacey? I bet Stacey hated that movie. What did you get Stacey for her birthday?*

"Dude, that was fifteen years ago!" Alan said. "And you weren't even there. You were interviewing for the sales manager position."

"Exactly. But if I *had* been here, *I* would've been the one, and you'd be behind this desk envying the crap out of *me*."

Outside, Gina could overhear Rick from where she was sitting and snapped her pencil. Another salesman came by with a lease contract and stood at her desk.

"What?" she said.

When he saw the expression on her face, he pivoted and took off the other way.

"Buddy, you are obsessed," Alan said, halfway out the door of Rick's office.

"Yeah, I am. And maybe if *you'd* been, she never woulda left you."

Alan stared at Rick, then at the governor's photo on his desk. Rick's eyes widened. As Alan grabbed the frame, Rick climbed over the desk and leapt onto his back, riding him like a Qatarian camel jockey. Alan struggled to open the frame, with Rick wildly grabbing for it. He reached behind and smashed it on Rick's head. *Boy, that felt good!* Rick slid off limply as Alan tore away the governor's photo, revealing a second photo of Stacey in cute little shorts and a tight halter top. Alan remembered Rick had taken that picture at a barbecue he'd hosted at his home five years earlier.

"I think you're going to need more ice, Rick," Alan said.

Rick lunged and grabbed Alan by the crotch. As Alan screamed, Rick snatched the photo and ran into the show-room. Alan chased his boss, who bobbed and weaved nimbly, dangling the photo and cackling. Sales people and customers watched in silent shock, some of them positive they were being punked and searching for the hidden cameras.

"I have an even bigger copy in my bedroom!" Rick said, laughing like a lunatic.

Suddenly, a stainless steel coffee mug hit Rick in the temple with the force of a line drive to center field. He went down. Getting on top of him, Alan tried to choke the life out of his former employer.

"Stop it, you're killing him!" Gina said.

As the two men pulled at the photo, it ripped in half. Both became enraged and pummeled each other like Battle-Bots. Gina and two other salesmen struggled to pull Alan and Rick off each other. Seeing his chance, Rick bolted outside onto the lot, where two burly drivers were about to unload brand-new SUVs from an enormous car carrier.

Still holding his half of the photo, Rick stood at the rear of the car carrier, rotating his hips and waving the photo.

"What's that noise?" one of the drivers said.

Wiping blood from his lip, Alan stood there, looking at Rick as if he were a mental patient.

"You know what?" he said. "I don't even care anymore, Rick. Go ahead and sue me."

"Oh, I plan to!"

Rick noticed a shiny new penny on the ground and bent down to get it. Straightening up, he showed it to Alan.

"Hey, Mr. Contest Winner! Wanna see your prize?"

Disgusted, Alan turned to leave, when a steel cable

holding the topmost SUV snapped. The vehicle rolled off tail-first and crushed Rick where he stood.

"Rick!" Gina said.

As screaming witnesses scattered like mice at a Japanese Catgirl convention, she charged toward the vehicle, which was now resting upside-down, and tried to find her dead boss—the love of her life—underneath the wreckage.

"Huh," the larger of the two drivers said. "I coulda swore I checked that."

Suddenly, Gina became enraged and kicked the SUV until her foot was bloody.

"You son of a bitch!" she said. "And to think I waited all these years! I hope you burn in hell, Rick Van Loon! Do you hear me under there? BURN IN HELL!"

In shock, Alan watched as two sympathetic bystanders helped to lead a weeping Gina Wallace away from the carnage and decided it would be better if he didn't attend the funeral.

"All I want to do is graduate from high school, go to Europe, marry Christian Slater, and die."

— BUFFY THE VAMPIRE SLAYER (1992)

In the dining room of the Black Hollow Inn, Sam and another guest named Zach interviewed the caretaker and his wife.

"He was a small child," she said, trying to hold back the tears. "So delicate and happy. He brought us such joy."

"I'm sorry," Sam said. "His death must have been a great loss."

The caretaker got to his feet. "This is enough." He took his wife's hand and led her away.

"Wait," Zach said. "You had *two* sons."

The old man froze, turned around, and gave Zach a stare worthy of a Reaper. But Zach didn't flinch. Sam looked at Kate and took her hand.

"Hank, the youngest," Zach said. "And *Charlie.*"

"We don't say his name," the caretaker said, his tone a dark warning.

Zach ignored the old man. "But isn't Charlie the one who pushed Hank into the well? Isn't that why he was sent away to the asylum?"

"I won't have you speak of him in this house!" the caretaker's wife said. "I died that day!"

MATT, Phoebe, Mom, and I stood behind the camera, watching the replay of the dining room scene on the video monitor. At the end, we heard Matt say, "Cut." Onscreen, the second AC, using a clapboard, created a tail slate. Wow, check out the movie lingo!

Matt turned to Uri. "I think we're good."

"Okay, people, let's prep for the next set-up!" Phoebe said.

As the crew moved around the set, I followed with my camcorder. After I got what I wanted, I joined Mom.

"How exciting is this?" I said.

"Pretty awesome!"

I heard a toilet flush, followed by a door slamming. Louie, looking pissed off, walked up to Phoebe and Matt, who were in the middle of a conference with Bailey. I had a feeling this might be good, and hit the RECORD button.

"I'm on a flight to Heathrow tomorrow night. Deal with it."

As a garnish—or is it *flourish*?—he pushed my camcorder away and strode off, almost knocking me over.

"And get that camera out of my face!"

"Hey!" Mom said.

Later in Jade's room, we crowded around the edit bay monitors as Jade took us through one of the sequences.

"I'm still having trouble with this part," she said.

She ran the scene where Kate is getting out of the shower and Sam surprises her. Jade freeze-framed on Kate's reaction.

"It's kind of cute?" she said. "But it doesn't pop."

"I think it works," Matt said.

Phoebe shook her head. "No, Jade's right. It needs something."

"Why don't you have her see the killer instead of Sam?" someone behind us said.

When we turned around, Dad was standing at the door, smiling like the Cheshire Cat.

"Dad!"

Giggling, I ran over and buried my face against him. Smiling, Mom stood a ways off with her arms folded.

"I take a few days off and already it's falling apart?" He winked at his brother, who looked away sheepishly.

"Dad, we have a major problem," I said.

Mom joined us. "Louie's bailing on us."

He looked at Phoebe and Matt. "That's not good. What are our options?"

"There's no other way," Matt said, shaking his head. "We have to kill off his character."

"I told you, I hate that idea," Phoebe said. "It ruins the ending."

"What else can we do?"

"How about if we double him?"

"A fake Shemp? No, it'll never work. Besides, who do we know that even looks like him?"

"Guys, let's settle down," Dad said. "We'll think of something."

Phoebe covered her face with her hands. "Without Louie, we're doomed."

DAD HAD ARRANGED for Mrs. Tessenbaum to look after Ed while he was away. Apparently, her Yorkie was a girl named Abby, and Ed was officially in love. We had gotten back our old adjoining rooms, which was a relief to me because it reminded me of his apartment. It sort of ticked Mom off at first, then she got used to it.

Phoebe and I sat in my room, working on my never-ending machinima project. She had thought it would be cool to create a machinima title sequence for the movie, and wanted to learn everything she could.

"Have you thought any more about who can Shemp for Louie?" I said.

"No. Besides, Matt said no way."

Using the touchpad, she moved around the canvas on the screen.

"This has such a creepy quality," she said. "Remind me to hire you for my next project."

It was time for a break and, opening the adjoining door, we saw Dad giving himself a once-over in the mirror. He was wearing his stupid avocado green silk shirt.

"I'm off," he said.

I blocked his exit, my arms folded across my chest. "That's what you're wearing?"

"What? This is a nice shirt."

"It looks like the tableside guacamole at El Cholo." No reaction. "Dad, put on one of your cool black shirts. With the pearl gray jacket. Oh, and those black shoes I like."

"I don't get what's wrong with this outfit."

He looked to Phoebe for sympathy, but she avoided eye contact. Yanking out his shirt tails, he slunk over to the closet, found what he was looking for, and turned back to us.

"Want to watch me change?"

"It's amazing they can even function," I said, closing our door.

Phoebe nodded. "Seriously."

MATTEI'S TAVERN WAS CROWDED. The elegant, comfortable restaurant overlooked a beautiful green lawn. Colored lights twinkled in the surrounding oaks and palms. Alan and Stacey sat at a cozy outside table, enjoying a local red they had tried at the bar.

"You look nice," she said.

"You can thank your fashion-conscious daughter."

"I was just thinking about the first time we met. We were at a restaurant like this. You said I reminded you of—"

"Grace Kelly."

"Only prettier," they said together.

They laughed, trying not to gaze into each other's eyes. Stacey had never been so nervous, and wondered if she should've worn her black pencil skirt instead of the apricot summer dress she had picked out.

"She was a classic," he said. "You know, I—"

"Oh no, you're not about to say something to ruin the mood, are you?"

"Me? Hey, I'm just happy to be alive."

"Alan, seriously. I want to thank you for doing this."

"What are we doing exactly?"

"Making a movie."

"I have to say—"

"Uh-oh, mood alert!"

"No, it's a compliment. I hope. I was going to say, this is the last thing I would've expected from you."

"Really?"

"You were always more responsible than me, Stace. More together."

"Was I?"

"Yes. Which is why I think Ruby is such a great kid. When I was her age, I didn't have half her smarts."

"Thank you. But you've done a lot for her, too."

"Not true, but thanks."

"It *is* true. You're there for her, Alan. A lot of men disengage after the split. She looks up to you."

"It's true, I am tall. Getting back to *you*, though, I can't figure out what you're doing up here."

"I don't know," she said. "I'm not as together as you might think. Then, this whole thing with Warren... I guess I wanted us to spend time as a family again."

"Testing the waters?"

"Maybe."

"Me, too. After that business with Rick, I—"

"I still can't believe he's dead."

"Me either. Guess they'll be looking for a new sales manager."

"You should apply."

"I don't know..."

Stacey sat quietly, tilting her glass back and forth. She watched dreamily as the wine coated it red and ran down in tiny rivulets.

"Stace, I really feel—" He became silent, chewed his thumb, and concentrated on the lights in the distance.

"What were you going to say?" Her voice was soft and expectant.

"No, nothing. Hey, how about a toast?" They raised their glasses. "To children."

As they touched their glasses together and drank, a server appeared with their filets. He put Stacey's down first.

"Careful, ma'am, the plate is very hot. Sir?"

Setting Alan's down, the server winked at Alan. Then, he placed a small gravy boat next to Stacey's food.

"What's this?" she said, sniffing the white fluffy substance. "It smells like—"

Dad winked at the waiter. "I thought you'd prefer your icing on the side this time."

She laughed and pretended to throw it at him. "You nut."

Inside in the lounge, several of the actors from the movie sat around the fireplace, drinking and chatting. Louie and Tara were on a sofa, going at it like a married couple.

"I was not hogging the scene," he said.

"You totally were! Even Bailey said you were stepping on my lines."

"I was trying to make it sound like a real conversation."

"Next time, try it with a British accent."

Disgusted, Louie got up and walked over to the bar. Instead of sports, the TV was tuned to a soap opera. The sound was muted, and the closed captioning was on.

"Whatever lager you have on draft," he said to the bartender. "Hey, is this *Roadside Hospital*?"

Sipping his beer, Louie watched the tense scene in the hospital room where Keely, the girl in a coma, was being visited by her parents. The mother was weeping and holding her child's hand while the father looked on stoically. Then, a young, good-looking doctor walked in, carrying a chart.

"Aw, man! This was supposed to be my part," Louie said. Then to the bartender, "Excuse me, can you turn up the sound?"

The bartender complied, and Louie could hear distinctly the actor speaking in a cultured British accent.

"The prognosis isn't good, I'm afraid," the doctor said to the parents. "Keely may never regain consciousness. At this stage, I would advise you to consider calling a priest straightaway."

The piano and strings swelled. Cut to Louie's mouth-wash commercial. Rather than fighting a scary CG dragon, the knight was now waving his sword threateningly at a cheesy cartoon. Shaking his head, Louie looked away.

The bartender switched the station to baseball. Louie looked over and noticed a red-headed woman in a midnight blue cocktail dress sitting next to him, sipping a Cosmo. He glanced back at Tara and shook his head. Absently, he used his finger to draw a frowny face on his beer glass.

"Why do women have to be so argumentative?" he said.

Laraine Moody turned to him and smiled. "My trouble is, I never argue." Then, extending her hand, "I'm Laraine."

"Hey, do I know you?"

"I dunno. Do you? *Louie?*"

He leaned back and looked her over carefully. There was something so familiar about her. Then, he recognized the distinctive mole on her neck.

"No way, it can't be. Larry?"

"Been a long time, buddy."

"Wh-what happened?"

"I made a few changes."

"But we were roommates for four years! I don't— Aw, man!"

"What?"

"We saw each other naked."

"Don't worry, you were never my type."

"Really?" Louie seemed disappointed. "What're you doing up here?"

"I'm performing."

"I remember. You always loved to sing jazz."

"What about you?"

"Me? Oh, I'm making this little movie. It's a student film. No big deal. I'm leaving tomorrow night for London. I got a small part in this indie—"

"Same ol' Louie," Laraine said, shaking her head. "In college, it was different. We didn't have to commit to anything. It was like we were in this nice little cocoon. Then, we get out in the real world, and what happens? Life kicks us in the teeth."

"Boy, does it ever."

"Look at me, Louie," Laraine said. "I've committed to something. It's hard. And it hurts."

"Oh, you mean... Did you, you know—"

"Don't be an idiot. The point is, I'm not giving up. I found my path. What's your excuse?"

Louie looked away and finished his beer. It wasn't anyone's business what he did with his life. Laraine took another sip of her Cosmo and checked her watch. Louie sneaked a peek at Tara, who was laughing uncontrollably.

"She really digs you," Laraine said.

"Where'd you hear that?"

"In the ladies' room." She got up. "I've got to get back onstage. Nice seeing you, Louie. Take care of yourself."

"Yeah, you, too, Larry— I mean, Laraine."

The bartender set down a fresh beer, courtesy of Laraine. As Louie sat there sipping it, he happened to make eye contact with Tara. She smiled in a way that made his eyebrows go up. And it occurred to him he was no longer thinking about London.

ALAN AND STACEY walked into the lobby of the B&B, smiling and talking. He wanted so much to take her hand, but was afraid of spoiling the evening. So, he kept his hands to himself.

Louie straggled in alone and shuffled over to them, acting like a kid who had just broken his neighbor's window with a baseball.

"I'm not flying out tomorrow," he said.

Alan glanced at Stacey. "Oh? That's great. I thought for sure we'd lost you. I mean, who could turn down Emma Watson? I know I couldn't."

Stacey gave him a playful jab to the ribs.

"Yeah, about that," Louie said.

He noticed Tara walking in with some of the other actors and lowered his voice.

"So, there is no other movie—I made the whole thing up. I, um, I have serious commitment issues. My analyst says it goes back to when my father ran off and joined a circus."

Alan guffawed at this unexpected humor.

"No joke, he joined an actual circus. He's their accountant."

"Sorry."

"And you know, the pay is better than I thought it would be."

"Louie, we appreciate you staying on board," Stacey said, touching his hand. "I know Phoebe and Matt will be thrilled."

"Thanks. Sorry about the thing with your daughter. See you on set."

They watched as he drifted away like a lost puppy. Tara caught up to him and, taking his arm, talked enthusiastically about their upcoming scenes.

"Wow," Alan said. "Actors."

Alan and Stacey came into his room quietly, and he tossed his jacket on the bed. She opened the connecting door to check on her daughter. Ruby was sound asleep, and Phoebe was sitting in a chair, going over the production schedule on her laptop. As Stacey tucked Ruby in and kissed her forehead, Phoebe got up quietly and came into Alan's room. Stacey followed, closing the door after her.

"Phoebe, thank you," Stacey said.

"Oh, it's no problem. She went right to sleep. How was dinner?"

"Nice," they said at the same time.

"Aha."

"Oh, good news!" Alan said. "Louie's not leaving tomorrow."

Phoebe hugged each of them. "Thank goodness! I was going crazy. I need to tell Matt. Did you guys want to come?"

"No, I'm a little tired," Stacey said.

Alan forced a yawn. "Me, too. We'll, uh, we'll see you in the morning."

"We have a production meeting at eight, don't forget."

"We'll be there."

"Good night."

After Phoebe left, Alan said, "Do you...want something to drink?"

He was nervous about being alone with Stacey. As a distraction, he went over to a nook in the wall and discovered a coffeemaker built for Thumbelina.

"I can make us some coffee," he said. "One thimble at a time."

"I don't want any."

"I could walk you back to your room."

"Are you throwing me out?"

"What? No!" She pointed to the connecting door. "No," he said in a stage whisper. "I'm not throwing you out."

"Good. It's funny how she'd rather be next to your room."

"Yeah, well, it's a tradition when we're on location."

"Okay, J.J. Abrams."

She took off her coat and sashayed over to the king bed. Then, she sat down, stroked the coverlet, and smiled at him.

"Such a big bed. They gave me a double." She pressed down on it. "Firm, too."

"I'm a little lost," he said. "Are you... Do you want me to—?"

She laughed, then quickly covered her mouth so as not to wake their daughter. "Why are men so thick?"

"We're visual learners. It's the reason they have all those hand signals in baseball."

"Alan, get over here." He moved to the bed and practically stood at attention.

"Sit," she said.

Again, he followed orders. She took his hand, intertwined her fingers with his, and looked into his eyes.

"Now, I want you to listen very carefully," she said, as if talking to a gibbering cretin.

He heard a creaking noise somewhere and turned to look. She grabbed his face and made him focus on her.

"What may or may not happen here tonight is not to be construed as anything other than what it is. You're to take it at face value."

"I don't know what you're saying."

"I'm feeling—"

"Hungry?" He got to his feet. "I have a mini-bar key. It's right—"

"No, I'm not hungry. For food."

The truth hit him like a bag of new nickels. "Ohh."

"All I'm saying is, *should* anything happen, I don't want you to think we're—"

"Oh no. Of course not. I mean, we're two adults who are married—to each other. And, and who happen to be alone in a hotel room together. On vacation."

"Alan, you're babbling."

"Who are incredibly attracted to each other in the worst way. Who, who both want to..." He became deadly serious. "I can do this."

She touched his face. Kissed him passionately on the lips and quickly got up. She crossed over to the connecting door, checked to make sure Ruby was still asleep, then bolted it. Turning back, she gave him a look of desire that could bring down a moose.

As their clothes flew off, he fumbled for the light and sank down on the bed with her in the sweet, comforting darkness.

"Batter up," she said.

23

"You guys gonna kill each other now?"

— CABIN FEVER (2002)

As Stacey slept contentedly, a hand gently brushed the hair from her face. She opened her eyes and saw Alan smiling hopefully. Smiling, too, she stretched, then took his hand and kissed it.

"I love you," he said.

"I love you, too."

"And I want another baby."

Suddenly, she felt as if someone had dropped an anvil on her chest.

"What? No, Alan. Let's not go to Stupidtown. Last night was wonderful, but—"

"Shh-shh. No, you'll see. I stayed awake all night thinking about this, and I finally figured it out."

"Alan, please don't."

"I can't believe it—the solution was right there all along. Are you listening? Okay, here it is."

He sat on the bed and took both her hands in his. She was fully awake now and knew in her soul he was about to destroy what precious little they had with a sledgehammer.

"You can work out of the house," he said. "Huh? Am I a genius?"

She sat up, her face and neck burning. *"What?"*

"Sure. That way, everybody gets what they want. Don't you see?"

She wished she had a severed limb so she could beat him into silence with it. Unaware of what she was thinking, he kept smiling.

"Leave," she said. "Alan, leave *now*."

Confused, he got up. "But I thought—"

"Dad?"

It was Ruby. He looked at the connecting door, then at Stacey.

"Leave," she said.

"Hang on, Rube! I-I'm coming!"

As he went into their daughter's room through the connecting door, Stacey punched her pillow. Everything came back to her like a dead body falling out of a closet. And she thought about that dreadful night a year earlier.

Alan was slumped on a bar stool at the kitchen counter of their home in Encino, rubbing his temples as Stacey angrily loaded the dishwasher.

"You had no right," she said, seething.

"It was taking up space in the garage. How long were you planning to hang onto it?"

"I don't know, Alan. Do dreams have an expiration date?"

"Stace, everyone has dreams. But this is our life. Why don't we focus on that for a change?"

She couldn't respond. How could she have married

someone so thoughtless? Her mother had warned her about car salesmen, but did she listen?

"If we ever do have another baby, I'll buy a new crib," he said. "What's the big deal?"

"You had no right."

Alan had retreated to the home office where, presumably, he was busy editing his home movies. Stacey had gone to see their daughter. As she approached Ruby's bedroom, she heard voices. Standing in the doorway, she watched as Ruby Skyped with Claire and Diego on her computer.

"He really stepped in it this time," she said.

Diego moved closer to the camera. "I don't see what the big deal is."

"That's because you're a guy," Claire said. Then to Ruby, "She might forgive him, you know."

Ruby tried making her voice sound lower. "'Be careful, Mrs. Smith! He's not the man you married.'"

"Is that from *Fido*?" Claire said.

Ruby shook her head. "Guys, I know he's my dad and all, but that was a major dick move."

The next morning, Stacey watched from her bedroom window as Alan threw the last of his stuff into his car. The rear window was completely blocked with his things, and she worried he wouldn't be able to see. She noticed Ruby walking out onto the driveway, wearing her pajamas and the pink bunny slippers Alan had bought her as a gag. He smiled and gently wiped away her tears. Then, they hugged. The bedroom window was open, and she could hear them talking.

"Everything will be fine," he said.

"Promise?"

Long after Alan had left, Stacey stared out the kitchen window at nothing. On the stove, water boiled over, drowning out the blue-orange flames that were like spirits who had never been born.

THE LAST DAYS of shooting were like a crazy blur to Stacey. She couldn't stop thinking about what an idiot Alan had been. Either he truly hadn't understood anything, or he was intentionally sabotaging any chance they might have had to get back together.

What started out as a family adventure had become a death march. It was all she could do to get through the long days. It was especially hard when they had to be in the same room together as they reviewed the dailies with Phoebe and Matt. During those difficult periods, she made herself focus on the work and on her daughter. She even pretended to be happy, for Ruby's sake. And Ruby did seem happy working on the movie. Stacey didn't want to spoil things. She told herself she could get through this.

For his part, Alan made the best of it. There were so many times he wanted to have it out with Stacey. At this point, he felt he had nothing left to lose. Hadn't she seen how much he wanted them back together? How he had figured out a way for them to make things work? Why else would he have swallowed his pride and returned to the place where Matt had betrayed him? That's what hurt the most—getting zero credit for forgiving his brother. It was painful when he had to be near Stacey, on set and during editing. Better to focus on the work and on Ruby. The only thing he wanted now was for his daughter to be happy.

24

"With endless love, we left you sleeping. Now we're sleeping with you. Don't wake up."

— 28 Days Later

At night in the garden it was pouring rain. Lightning flashed, turning the sky white-hot. Sam and Zach were fighting next to the well. As they struggled, it was clear Zach was trying to push Sam down the hole. But Sam had the upper hand.

"Charlie and I grew up together," Zach said.

Sam stared into the blackness of the abyss. "So *you* killed Hank."

"It was an accident!"

Zach managed to pull away and backed off as Sam watched him warily.

"We were playing a game when Hank fell in. I got scared and ran away. Charlie didn't even try to defend himself, so he got blamed. When I was old enough, I took a job at the asylum to be near him."

"You helped him escape?"

"What was I supposed to do? He was my best friend!"

Sam took a swing and hit Zach in the jaw, knocking him down. He tried getting away, but Zach grabbed his leg, then kicked Sam in the stomach. With incredible strength, he picked Sam up and tried forcing him down the well. Grimacing, Sam clung to the edge as he dangled helplessly over the bottomless void.

Kate and the caretaker's wife appeared just as Sam was losing his grip. Desperate to save her husband, Kate picked up a shovel and smashed Zach in the skull. He turned around, wavering and glassy-eyed, touching the back of his head and finding blood. Seeing their chance, the two women helped free Sam. Zach vomited and, losing his balance, fell backward into the well, his scream echoing. Then, silence.

Sam and Kate hugged tightly and kissed each other's face.

"I was so scared!" she said. "I almost lost you."

"I'm not going anywhere. By the way, where'd you learn to use a shovel?"

They kissed passionately. The caretaker's wife pointed to the inn, her eyes wild with panic.

"Look!" she said.

As the rain beat down, the inn went up in flames. On the roof, two vague figures were locked in combat. The caretaker and Chainsaw Chuck were going at it with chainsaws as the inn burned out of control. Below, the caretaker's wife, Sam, Kate, and the other guests watched, transfixed.

The killer came at his father, viciously going for his neck but gouging his shoulder instead. Screaming, the caretaker swung his weapon at his son, slicing him across the chest. Tumbling backward, Chainsaw Chuck fell off the roof and impaled himself on the wrought iron fence below. With a horrendous creak, a section of the inn collapsed in a ball of fire and sparks as the caretaker leapt off the roof in a desperate attempt to save himself.

Sam, Kate, and the caretaker's wife hurried to where the old man lay dying. Together, they dragged him away from the roaring flames and onto the grass. Barely conscious, he was bleeding out. The old woman took his hand. He spoke to her through spit-up blood.

"I remember," he said. "You were a girl, young and beautiful. One more dance..."

Sam knelt and examined the caretaker. "He's gone. I am so sorry."

Wailing miserably, the caretaker's wife got to her feet. "No!"

Hysterical, she backed away from the inferno as Sam and Kate looked on in pity. Blindly, she ran through the darkness and the rain. She failed to notice the open well and before she could stop fell in without a sound.

As the sun broke through the heavy clouds of smoke and ash, firefighters continued spraying water on the cooling embers of the wrecked inn. Rays of beautiful golden light illuminated the place where it had once stood. Dazed survivors waited as police and EMTs examined them for injuries and smoke inhalation.

Gently, Sam covered Kate with a gray fleece blanket and put his arm around her as she shivered, staring at the remains of their honeymoon.

"'We should have gone to Sunny Beach like I told you,'" he said.

"Wait, is that from *Dead Snow*?"

"I thought it was appropriate."

As the house lights came up in the Roger Corman Theater at the Pink School, Claire, Diego, and I got to our feet, screaming and catcalling with everyone else in the audience —including Mom and Dad. Matt, who was wearing a gray Chambray fedora, stood on the stage with Phoebe, holding a microphone and doing his best to speak over the crazy applause. He kept pushing down an imaginary wave with his hands, but no one wanted to stop. Using her fingers, Phoebe let out a shrill whistle, and we finally settled down.

"I want to thank Jade for turning this piece of junk into an actual movie," Matt said. "Jade?"

More screaming and stamping of feet as our brilliant editor stood in the front row, small and petite and barely visible. From where we stood, I could see her blushing while we chanted in unison.

"Jay-UD! Jay-UD!"

"I also want to thank my producer Phoebe for not giving up on me," Matt said. "Now, I know I come off as a little rude sometimes—"

"Noooooo," everyone said.

Laughing self-consciously, he hugged Phoebe hard and kissed her—surprising her—as people chanted again.

"Phoe-BE! Phoe-BE!"

Phoebe grabbed the mic. "And I want to thank Alan and Stacey Navarro."

"And Ruby!" I said.

"We could've never done it without you guys!"

Shielding her eyes with her hand, Phoebe stared out into the crowd.

"There they are!" she said.

Matt gestured. "Come on, get up here!"

Thundering applause and foot stomping roared as Mom and Dad looked at each other, unsure of what to do.

"Go on!" I said.

They both stood awkwardly, but didn't make any attempt to move. I forced them to take a bow and tried pushing them together so they'd at least look like a couple. They smiled and waved mechanically as Phoebe and Matt pressed their hands together and bowed like Tibetan monks.

Later, when the five of us walked out to the film school parking lot, we saw Phoebe talking on her phone.

"We're looking to have the score finished in a few weeks," she said. "And we're still waiting for some CG shots. Oh yeah, we had a problem with the model, so we'll need to burn down the inn again."

Claire and Diego were talking excitedly about the movie, but I was watching Matt as he sneaked up behind Phoebe and slipped his hands around her waist. Almost dropping her phone, she swung around, and he kissed her in the sweetest way I had ever seen. I had no idea what had gotten into my uncle, but he was acting like a real person. When I turned around, I saw my parents watching, too, both a little sad.

"I'm going to the car," Mom said.

Dad went up to Phoebe and Matt. She hugged him. Then, he gave Matt a bear hug.

"Easy, dude," Matt said.

"You did good, little bro."

"Alan, I appreciate everything—I can't even tell you. Phoebe and I have been working on this thing for over two years. I still can't believe we finished it. Sorry about, you know, not being upfront with you."

Dad nodded. "If you do make it to the majors, I wouldn't try pulling that one again."

"I know this wasn't the movie you wanted," Phoebe said. "But I hope you and Stacey can maybe…"

Dad shook his head. "It's a very good movie. And I think we've done everything we can. It's up to God now. We'd better go."

"Coming to the wrap party?" Matt said.

"Wouldn't miss it."

Phoebe's phone went off again. "See you!" she said. Then into her phone, "Hello? Hey!"

Dad put his arm around me as we headed out with Claire and Diego. "I'm starving. How about some burgers?"

Mom, Dad, and I stood next to her car outside the apartment building, after having dropped Claire and Diego so they could get ready for the party. Mom planned to go home to change and promised to meet us there. I was a little bummed because I had wanted us to drive over together.

"I can't believe summer's almost over," I said.

Dad looked at Mom. "I'll have her back Sunday night."

Mom hugged and kissed me. "Bye, sweetie. See you tonight."

"Bye, Mom," I said and slung my backpack over my shoulder. "Wait, I almost forgot! Mom, I need to show you both something real quick."

"Honey, I have to get going."

Dad gave my shoulder a squeeze. "Can't we see it tomorrow?"

"No-uh! Please? It's super important!"

Mom and Dad exchanged a parental glance, and I knew I had won.

In the living room, I finished hooking up my laptop to the flat screen while Mom and Dad sat apart on the loveseat, with Ed lying between them. Well, at least they were occupying the same piece of furniture.

"Is this your machinima project?" Mom said, yawning. "Sorry, I'm really tired."

"This won't take long, I promise. No, it's some of the stuff I shot with my camcorder while we were making the movie. I thought we could use it as part of the bonus material on the Blu-ray disk."

"Thinking ahead," Dad said. "That's my girl."

I grabbed the remote, dimmed the lights, and stood off to the side, saying a silent prayer this scheme of mine would work. Then, I hit PLAY. Now, admittedly, I'm better with machinima than I am with a camcorder, but even I was impressed with the quality of the HD footage that appeared in glorious widescreen.

Instead of scenes from the making of *Chainsaw Honeymoon*, all of the images were of Mom, Dad, and me. And, yes, it was a home movie. Claire and Diego had helped me find the perfect music. We ended up agreeing on "Someone Like You." Not the Adele song. This one was by some guy I had never heard of—Van Morrison?

Anyways, thanks to Jade, the scenes worked. Mom and Dad laughing. Me being chased by the killer. Mom and Dad working together on the shooting script. Me doing a dramatic death scene by the well. Mom and Dad talking intimately between takes in the garden when all of a sudden I leap out, dressed as Chainsaw Chuck. Mom and Dad enjoying their intimate dinner at Mattei's Tavern. Mom and Dad about to kiss.

I ended my movie with the recording I'd made of Mom telling the story of how she and Dad had met. Then, I freeze-framed on her smiling face. When it was over, I brought the lights back up. Mom was crying, and Dad was pretending not to. Always prepared, I handed each of them some tissues.

"Thank you," Mom said.

Dad wiped his eyes. "I don't understand. How did you get us at dinner?"

"Phoebe bribed one of the servers. It was all part of the plan."

Mom blew her nose. "Ruby, I don't know what to say."

I switched off the TV. "Oh, look at the time! We have to get ready for the party."

I shooed them like naughty dogs who knew they weren't supposed to be on the furniture.

"Come on—chop chop, people!"

I DON'T REQUIRE a lot of makeup. Less is more, I always say. On the other hand, I was going to my first wrap party. Urban Decay to the rescue! A surprise summer rain had cooled everything down by evening. Phoebe had arranged to hold the event on a soundstage at the Pink School. Claire and Diego were already there when the three of us arrived, waving at us near the entrance. I could hear the music blasting from inside, and couldn't wait to go in.

Just for grins, I had brought along Ed. I felt like he needed to get out more, and Mom had signed up to hold his leash. I hugged my friends and we went inside. The place looked incredible. The ceiling was adorned with black and gray balloons and crepe paper streamers. Cardboard cutouts of red chainsaws hung everywhere. Drywall sections on rollers stood at the edges, smeared with blood. And in bloody letters, REDRUM. And the food—oh my gosh! Beef sliders, beef satay, shredded beef tacos. I didn't know where to start.

Everyone had come. I had decided to wear my most comfortable red high-top Converse for the occasion. And it was a good thing, too, because I had never danced so much in my life.

Later while laughing and dancing with Claire, I looked over and saw Diego on the side, sipping Martinelli's and watching the crowd.

"He's so into you," Claire said. "You know that, right?"

"What? You're crazy. We're just friends."

"Sure, whatever you say."

"Claire!"

"Ruby, you're the smartest person I know. But you are also the dumbest. Maybe you need to watch less horror and more rom-com."

As she stared at Diego, it dawned on me what was really going on.

"This isn't about me—it's about *you*," I said.

"What?"

Claire was a terrible poker player—the worst. We used to play on her mom's kitchen table. Whenever she would get any good cards, she would roll her eyes and giggle. I could read her like the big print edition of *Reader's Digest*.

"You're in love with him," I said. "Don't deny it, Claire. You've been in love with Diego since—"

"Since I can remember. But it's not me he loves, Ruby. It's *you*. And you're too stupid and blind to—"

Claire ran off before she could finish, leaving me standing on the dance floor with my mouth hanging open.

One of the decorations fell, barely missing her. When I turned around, I saw Diego walking toward me just as the DJ put on "Sometime Around Midnight." And that's when I saw my friend differently. I stood there in a daze, and as he took my hand to dance, it felt like the most natural thing in the whole world. If this was heaven, then kill me now.

When the song ended, Diego went to get me a soda. I happened to look up and noticed a mannequin dressed as Chainsaw Chuck suspended from the ceiling. It looked so real. Good job, Phoebe! Then, disaster. The wire holding it up snapped, and the creature came crashing down on me before I could get away, knocking me to the floor.

When I opened my eyes, I found Diego kneeling next to me.

"You okay?" he said, helping me to my feet.

"I think so. My head hurts."

"Maybe you hit it on the floor when you fell."

"No, it was the thing on the—"

A woman screamed. I saw the crowd parting, looks of terror on their faces as Chainsaw Chuck leaped down from the ceiling, his hat pulled low, his duster billowing. At first, I thought this was a prank. *Ha ha, Matt. Very funny.* But he revved his chainsaw and drove it into Uri's back. In seconds, it burst through his chest. As real blood squirted every-where, the music stopped and people ran. Grabbing Diego's hand, I looked to see where my parents were, but I couldn't find them.

More screaming split the air as the killer cut a bloody human path toward us.

"No, it can't be," I said. "You're not real!"

Everything slowed. The noise melted into a high-pitch whine as Phoebe and Matt, his black top hat flying off, grabbed Chainsaw Chuck's duster and tried dragging him away from his next victim. With the grace of a dancer, the monster swung the chainsaw around and cut both of them down. Out of nowhere, Mom and Dad appeared. Dad was clutching a metal folding chair as Mom stood behind him, terrified, still holding Ed on his leash, the dog jumping and barking.

Diego tried pulling me away to safety, but I couldn't move. I watched as Dad raised the chair and bashed Chainsaw Chuck on the back of his head, knocking him down and sending the bloody weapon skittering across the floor. It stopped at my feet. I looked at Diego, then at the chainsaw. I wasn't sure what to do, but I wasn't going to let this murderous lunatic harm my parents. So, I picked up the weapon.

Time returned to normal. Chainsaw Chuck was on his feet and had my parents by the throat—one in each hand— as Ed barked nonstop and tried to bite the attacker. I revved the chainsaw to get his attention. He swung around and stared at me, his soulless eyes like brilliant white diamonds.

"Stay away from my family!" I said.

Revving the chainsaw again, I walked toward him. He saw the tableau of frozen faces, then me, and released my parents. Both sank to the ground, gasping for air. Chainsaw Chuck flung the dog aside with his boot and ran away, disappearing into the shadows. This needed to end, so I went after him.

"Ruby, no!" Mom said.

Dad tried grabbing me as I passed, but I kept going.

I didn't have any idea what had gotten into me, but I knew I had to do this. I discovered an exit at the back of the soundstage, which led to a dark corridor. When I entered it, I couldn't hear anything but the sound of the chainsaw idling in my hand. At the end of the corridor, I could just make out a shadowy figure the size of a man. Gripping my weapon, I marched toward it.

As I passed a doorway, a body blow flung me violently across the corridor and into a wall. Vaguely, I saw the chainsaw sitting in the middle of the floor, too far for me to reach. I tried to focus, and I realized the thing I saw earlier was actually a huge movie poster of the bloodthirsty female star of *La Llorona and the Quarterback* from American Worldwide Pictures.

Ed had found me and was licking my hand. I heard a scrape. He growled viciously. As I looked up, I saw Chainsaw Chuck picking up the weapon. He examined it, then held it at his side as he approached me. This was it. I was alone with the crazed killer I created. As I prepared to die, random sights and smells flew through my brain. I thought of my parents. All I had ever wanted was for them to be together. I thought of Diego. How could I have been such an idiot? Well, it didn't matter now. Claire would look after him.

I stared at the blurry image of the demon standing before me; he raised the chainsaw. Ed tore viciously at his duster, but he ignored the dog and concentrated only on me. I closed my eyes, waiting for the end.

"Everything will be fine," Chainsaw Chuck said.

Nothing but blackness now and a far-off clicking noise. I became aware of muddled voices and what sounded like a PA system. *Nurse Collins to the nurses' station. Nurse Collins to the nurses' station...*

"God brought us together for a reason. This is it."

— THE CONJURING

When I opened my eyes, I found myself lying in a raised-up bed with rails in an unfamiliar white room—a hospital room! I looked over and saw that the clicking I'd heard was coming from one of the machines I was hooked up to. Mr. Shivers was sitting on the credenza, watching me. *How had he gotten here?* Groaning, I tried sitting up.

Mom approached the bed. "Thank God!" she said, taking my hand.

Dad, who was standing opposite her and acting all emotional, laid his hand on my arm. "Hi, baby."

My body was stiff and my head was bandaged. I felt so groggy—and nauseous. It was hard for me to concentrate on my surroundings. I had no clue how long I'd been here, and I was scared of finding out. I mean, what if this was like that

Keely girl in *Roadside Hospital*, and I had actually been in a coma for, like, a year!

"How long have I been here?"

"A few days," Mom said.

Thank God!

"Ruby, do you remember the party?"

"Yes, I... Diego and I were dancing. Then, something fell on me and—"

"It was a stupid decoration," Dad said. "It knocked you out cold. By the way, Phoebe feels horrible and blames herself."

"What? But I remember getting up and— Chainsaw Chuck! He was *real*, and he started killing people! And I was so worried about protecting both of you. I, I chased him. He was going to kill me, but..."

"Ruby, honey," Mom said. "You were unconscious. Then, the ambulance came and brought you here."

"What? No, I remember. Where's Ed? Is he okay?"

"He's fine—he's at home," Dad said.

I tried wrapping my head around the fact that what I thought had happened was only a dream. None of it—the blood, the screaming—was real. Which, I guess, was a good thing because it meant Matt and Phoebe—and Uri—were still alive.

"You can't even imagine what I've been through," I said.

"Ruby, we need to tell you something." Mom was smiling and looking at Dad.

"And the whole time I kept thinking, all I wanted was for us to be a family again." Great, now I was crying like a feeb.

"We *are* a family," Mom said.

"No-uh, I mean a *real* family."

"That's what she's trying to tell you, Rube," Dad said,

reaching across the bed and taking Mom's hand. "We're back together."

"Wait, what?"

Smiling and crying, Mom showed me her wedding ring. I couldn't believe it, and had to touch her finger as proof.

"When I saw you lying on the floor, I thought I'd lost you," he said. "It made me realize what an idiot I was."

"We both were," she said, kissing his hand. Then to me, "We love you so very much, honey. You are the most precious thing in our lives. Your dad and I are going to figure it out, but this time we'll do it together."

"He told me everything would be fine."

"Who told you?" Mom said.

"Chainsaw Chuck. Look, it doesn't even matter."

The sudden sound of a chainsaw outside startled me, and I had to keep myself from screaming. Maybe this was another stupid dream within a dream, and I only *thought* I'd woken up. *Please don't let the killer be outside!*

Dad walked over to the window and looked out. "Huh. Looks like they're still working on that dead tree in the parking lot."

A smiling nurse with cornrows appeared in the doorway. "Is our little girl awake? I'll get the doctor."

When she returned, a handsome doctor wearing Burberry glasses was with her. Grabbing a penlight from his pocket, he leaned in close to check my pupils. His breath smelled like Earl Grey tea.

"You are a very lucky young lady," he said in a British accent.

I gawped at him. "Seriously?"

"Not sure I understand," he said, turning to the nurse.

Mom laughed. "Welcome back, Ruby."

My eyes kept darting from one person to another, and

my brain struggled to put the pieces together as the doctor tried explaining to me that, because of swelling in my brain, they had put me into a medically induced coma. Then, as he discussed the next steps with my parents, I looked across the room and realized another patient had been in here with me all along.

A woman resembling Nadia Ionescu was lying in the other bed. She was speaking quietly with a man who, I kid you not, was a dead ringer for Klaus Becker and who was sitting next to her, holding her hand. Both were elderly. When she saw me looking at her, she smiled. Anyone could tell they were deeply in love.

THE GOOD NEWS IS, there was no permanent brain damage. Whew! And I still have two weeks of summer to look forward to. But even though I'm dying to see my friends, I feel like I need to stay close to home—near Mom and Dad. And Ed. We're planning a trip to Disneyland before school starts, and I can't wait! We're going to stay at the Grand Californian—best hotel on the property, if you ask me.

The accident had been bad and totally random. Still, one good thing did come out of it—I no longer slept like the dead. That's not to say I have trouble sleeping. I sleep fine now and wake up early every morning, excited about starting my day. At first, Mom didn't trust that this was a real thing. Eventually, though, she gathered up The Beggar's Sideshow stuff, stuck it in a box, and put it out in the garage. Everything except Mr. Shivers, who I insisted on keeping in my room as a reminder of what I'd been through.

It was night now, and I was in my own bed in my own house, with Ed sleeping on the floor next to me. Outside, a soft El Niño rain was coming down, streaking my window. Dad was sitting on the edge of the bed, like old times. He had a Blu-ray disc of *Nightbreed* in his hand. Apparently, he and Mom had made a deal. He would try watching more horror, if she would agree to watch a rom-com once in a while. I think her pick for tonight was *Bridesmaids*. Close enough.

"Good night, baby," Dad said. "Did you brush your teeth?"

"Yes. Dad, I love you."

"I love you, too. See you in the morning."

He kissed me and got up to leave as Mom walked into the room.

"What about me?" she said.

I'd never seen them so happy. Dad bent down, pretending his back hurt, and kissed Mom's tummy. Wow, a baby sister! Actually, it was way too early to tell what the sex would be, but I'd already decided I was having a little sister. I mean, come on. Who else could I possibly pass along all my wisdom to?

"I love you, too, Mom," I said.

"That's better. Good night, sweetie."

"Are you saying that to me or the baby?"

"You're both my sweeties."

Mom gave my bed a last tuck, kissed me, and joined Dad at the door. "Sure you're getting up early again tomorrow? I really miss that cowbell."

"I'll get up, I promise!"

"Sleep well," Dad said. Then, as they left the room, "Pancakes tomorrow!"

Snuggled tight in bed, I had started to drift off when I heard music outside. It sounded like "I Will Follow You Into The Dark." Was there a party going on somewhere? I wondered if I should call Dad. Cautiously, I climbed out of bed, approached the window, and looked down. I couldn't believe it.

Diego was standing in the rain, holding up a boom box and looking up at me, not unlike John Cusack in *Say Anything*. What was he trying to tell me with that song? Not caring if I got wet, I flung the window open and stuck my head out. The cool rain felt good on my face.

"Ruby, what's going on?" Mom said.

"Nothing!"

Mom had called to me from somewhere in the house. As soon as Diego heard her, he turned off the music.

"Hola," he said.

"Diego, what're you doing here?"

"You haven't told me how the story ends."

"Shh! You're loco, you know that? It ends happily ever after. Now, go home before you get sick and I have to bring you chicken soup."

"Then, I'll stay."

"Go!" I said, laughing.

As he turned to leave, I called to him.

"Diego? Thanks for the song. See you tomorrow, okay?"

"Hasta luego."

Then, he did something I'll never forget. He blew me a kiss. I don't want to get all Jack-and-Rose here, but my heart actually fluttered.

Watching him as he went off in the rain, I closed the window. I had been working on a video for my friends. Seeing Diego gave me an idea for a special ending—something that would be just for him. I gave Ed a pat on the head, grabbed my camcorder from the dresser, sat at my desk, smoothed my hair, cleared my throat, hit RECORD, and spoke into the camera.

"Someone—maybe a saint—once said, 'Happiness is not having what you want, but wanting what you have.' Every story needs a happy ending. It's why we get up every day, why we forgive the ones we hurt, why we're even alive. I'm not saying it's easy or permanent. But it doesn't mean we shouldn't try our best. I mean, what else can we do?"

Tomorrow, I planned on finishing up the video and playing it for Diego and Claire, so they would be able to hear the whole story from my perspective—everything I'd lived through this past summer. I hoped they would like it, especially Diego.

I put away the camcorder, climbed into bed, put in my earbuds, and fired up one of my faves—"Spirits" by The Strumbellas. Feeling very warm and very safe, I closed my eyes and let the music carry me away.

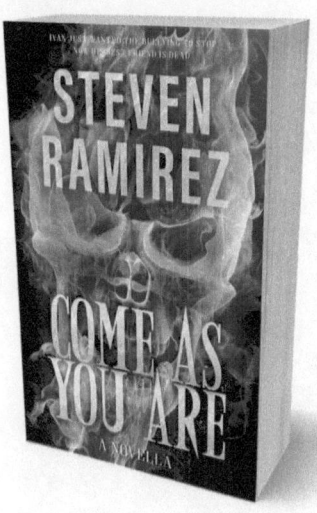

YOUR FREE BOOK IS WAITING

*Ivan just wanted the bullying to stop.
Now his best friend is dead.*

Download your free copy of the novella
Come As You Are. Then, turn on all the lights.

STEVENRAMIREZ.COM/GET-HORROR

ABOUT THE AUTHOR

Steven Ramirez is the award-winning author of thriller, supernatural, and horror fiction. A former screenwriter, he's written about zombie plagues and places infested with ghosts and demons. His latest novel is *Faithless*, a thriller. Steven lives in Los Angeles.

AUTHOR WEBSITE
stevenramirez.com

- facebook.com/byStevenRamirez
- instagram.com/byStevenRamirez
- twitter.com/byStevenRamirez
- goodreads.com/byStevenRamirez
- bookbub.com/authors/steven-ramirez